Malicious
INTENTIONS

D.C. ELMORE

Thirsty for more?

Explore
www.dcelmore.com

Global Book Publisher

Global Book Publisher

Edited by Rhea N. Lovan & Rupal T. Sojitra
Cover design by Rob Quillen

ISBN: 1-4196-0964-5

www.booksurge.com

Printed in the United States of America

For Rupal

...

You have brought me
indescribable happiness.

Malicious
INTENTIONS

Logon to www.dcelmore.com
for an interactive companion!

CHAPTER ONE

Five squad cars rocketed by the closed businesses and luxurious hotels that decorated the Atlantic Ocean beachfront. The screams of the sirens shattered the serenity of the city streets announcing that the keepers of the peace were on their way. The red and blue lights were beacons of hope pulsating through the darkness. Only responding to a dire emergency would warrant the Élan Police Department to partake in this Indy 500 style of driving and this call would not be the exception.

The evening shift officers exceeded speeds quite a few notches above the 100 mile per hour mark in streets with very little maneuvering room. Each had overheard the same cold hard facts dispatched over the radio. A possible murder scene had just been reported at the apartment complex at 1005 Oceanview Parkway. It also happened to be where one of Élan's best homicide detectives lived.

• • •

Usually, Homicide Detective Carmen Moore would have had her police scanner on. She would have heard the emergency tones and awakened long enough to get the gist of the call to see if her services would be required. However, tonight she had made the conscious decision to switch the police scanner off in celebration of the flawless arrest that was made earlier in the day. She came home, stripped off her clothes, put on her pajamas, and fell into bed quite content with having the next three days off.

Carmen and her partner had been working on an exhausting three month investigation into the disappearance and, inevitably, the murder of a downtown waitress. They had spent countless hours reviewing eyewitness testimonies and forensic evidential data collected from the woman's vehicle found abandoned beneath an overpass. Carmen had decided to re-interview the waitress' boyfriend and challenge the discrepancies that she had noticed in his alibi from his previous sworn statement. After an hour or so of listening to his lies, she asked him for a DNA sample in order to prove that it was not his skin that they had recovered from underneath the waitress' fingernails. He hesitated, but finally agreed. The DNA test came back with a positive match.

• • •

The late night shrill of the telephone did not penetrate the tranquility of Carmen's dreams. However, from underneath the bedspread her Chihuahua, Cuffs, poked his head out and peered into the darkness at the object ringing relentlessly. He climbed up onto her body and plopped his bottom down on her chest. He moved his determined little face down to hers and gently licked the tip of her nose. After several more unsuccessful attempts to wake her, he took his paw and began scratching at her pajama top with his short black nails.

Carmen's eyes fluttered and she patted Cuffs on the back to assure him that she was awake. She rose up onto her elbows and glanced at the alarm clock. Sighing, she lifted Cuffs from her chest and placed him gently on the pillow next to her. She lunged for the phone on the nightstand but found that the sheets were twisted around her legs in an almost paralyzing embrace. She tumbled onto the floor with a loud thud.

Carmen tried to kick her legs free for a few seconds before she noticed Cuffs looking down at her. He cocked his head from side to side as if wondering what she was now doing on the floor. His innocent face made her smile and she calmly unraveled her legs and reached up for the phone. "This is Detective Moore," she managed through a yawn.

"Carmen? Are you alright?" the deep scruffy voice demanded.

"Chris?" Carmen asked, bewildered by her partner's late night call. "What are you doing up at this hour? It's almost midnight."

"I was so worried when you didn't answer the phone right away," he stated. "What in hell took you so long?"

"I was sleeping, Chris," she remarked slightly annoyed.

"Look, there's a report of a 10-0 in apartment #5 of your building," he began. "I couldn't remember which apartment was yours and I started to worry that some revengeful scumbag took you by surprise."

Carmen said nothing for a moment as she struggled to comprehend Chris' words and formulate a response. It wasn't possible that someone had been killed in her building. Chris had to be pulling a fast one on her and she wasn't going to fall for it. "Are you drunk?" she finally retorted.

"No, I'm not drunk," Chris replied, understanding the reason for her unsavory attitude. "I'm only about a mile away from the complex. Can't you hear the sirens?"

Carmen fell silent and listened. The protective walls of emotional restraint raised into place as her ears picked up the familiar wails. "God Chris, this just can't be happening, not in my building," she said dismayed.

"I'm turning onto your street now," he replied. "Meet me downstairs and we'll see what twist of fate has been laid at our feet. Maybe it'll be a false alarm."

"Yeah, maybe," Carmen offered skeptically, her gut instinct already knowing the truth. "I'll see you in a few."

"Be careful," Chris urged. "If this really turns out to be a murder scene, the killer might still be in the building."

Carmen dropped the receiver back onto the cradle and took a deep breath to try to clear away the apprehension that had crept into her mind. She scrambled to her feet and hurried over to open the bedroom window. She peered down at the street below that was now cluttered with police cruisers. "This is unreal," she muttered.

Carmen rushed over to the closet and flipped on the light. She stripped off her pajamas and grabbed a faded pair of blue jeans that slipped easily over her strong, slim physique. Not bothering with a bra, she yanked a navy blue sweatshirt off a hanger and quickly pulled it over her head. She grabbed her worn black leather holster off the solid oak dresser and raced back over to the bed. She slipped her hand underneath one of the pillows and removed a Glock 40 from beneath it. She secured it in the holster and sprinted out of the bedroom. She grabbed her badge off the kitchen counter as she passed by and bolted out the front door.

• • •

Carmen hit the solid steel stairwell door with enough force to knock a well-built man down. She peered down the first flight of stairs half-expecting to see the killer running up it with almost super-natural speed, but she was alone. She felt vulnerable under the dimly lit stairwell lights that invoked shadows in every corner, but she refused to let fear guide her intuitive mind. She removed the Glock from the holster and flattened her back against the wall. She proceeded down the stairwell and scanned every crawlspace, crevice, and step as she descended. She searched for any sign of evidence that may have been dropped had the killer used the stairs for any reason.

When Carmen reached the base of the stairwell, she saw Officer Bryce Cooper standing in the entryway off the first floor. Cooper was six-foot four, had an impressive muscular build, and had no trouble holding his own. Surprisingly though, the look frozen on his face tonight actually startled her. For the past five years, she could not recall seeing him with such utter disbelief and horror raging on his face. But, duty called and he would understand her false indifference. "Are you alright?" she asked re-holstering her weapon.

"This one's pretty bad," Cooper replied with his sorrow-filled brown eyes glancing down at her. "I've never seen such a vicious attack on another person before, especially a woman."

"We have a job to do," Carmen said sternly, "so, get yourself together and come on."

As Carmen passed him, she gripped his shoulder and squeezed gently. She knew full well that there were no words for moments like these, just a quiet understanding. They had all seen things that would haunt their dreams for years to come. Yet, day after day, each officer on Élan's police force reported for duty not because they had to, but because they wanted to.

Carmen exited the stairwell and a sickening copper odor swirled in her nose. She was standing more than twelve feet away from apartment #5 and yet, she was completely engulfed in the smell of blood. She proceeded down the hallway toward the bright yellow tape draped around the outside perimeter of the apartment with the words 'Police Line: Do Not Cross' imprinted in bold black lettering. Like any crime scene, the area had been cordoned off by police personnel. Two officers were stationed outside the double doors that led into the apartment complex. Sgt. Hammond was standing just outside the door of apartment #5 monitoring access to the apartment and keeping a detailed log of which emergency personnel had entered the premises.

"We're glad you're okay," Sgt. Hammond announced as Carmen ducked underneath the crime scene tape.

"So am I," she replied with an easy smile. "Is Chris inside?"

"Yes ma'am, he is."

Chris Duhn was 5'10, stocky, with blue eyes and black wavy feathered hair. Well-educated and street smart, Chris was an excellent detective. He and Carmen had gone through the police academy together. They had helped each other excel in their studies and as a result became the best of friends. Now they were partners and complimented each other very nicely. Furthermore, he held no prejudices against her and that was a welcome relief for Carmen.

"Detective Moore, so nice of you to join us," Chris mused emerging from the crime scene in black slacks and a beige silk shirt. "We hate to drag you out of your nice cozy bed, but it seems that a detective's job is never done."

Carmen knew Chris only joked with her when the odds of seeing the crime scene were probably going to make her revisit her supper. Over time she had become accustomed to his 'make the mood a little lighter' tactic. "So, does this mean you're going to be sweet and handle this one on your own?" she inquired. "I mean you seem to have it all under control and I could really use a good night's rest."

Chris' gaze shifted from hers for a split second, and when he looked back she could see the sadness in his crystal blue eyes." I think you should stay awhile and lend me your expertise," he encouraged. "Besides, partner, you know you won't be able to go back to sleep anyway."

They both knew he was right. She would toss and turn thinking that someone may overlook or mishandle the one piece of evidence that would solve the case. Mishandling evidence could cause misleading results that might result in its inadmissibility in court. Sometimes, such mishaps allowed cold-blooded killers to go free. She figured in the long run if losing a little bit of sleep insured the integrity of her crime scene, it was worth it.

Carmen noticed that Cooper had emerged from the stairwell and she motioned him over. "Alright, this is what I want done," she instructed. "Cooper, call dispatch and get every available unit to assist. I want every occupant on this floor and the second floor interviewed. I also want the area canvassed and a thorough search done of the complex including the dumpster out back. If any evidence is located, have the officer contact one of the crime scene specialists immediately. They are on their way, right?"

"About three minutes away," Chris reported.

"Good," Carmen said. "Call the coroner and see if he'll come down. I want him to see the victim's body prior to us moving it."

"No problem," Cooper assured.

"Alright, let's get to it," Carmen urged, turning toward the open doorway.

Chris grabbed Carmen's sweatshirt and gave it a light tug. "Be prepared, okay?" he whispered. "I just took a quick glance and this isn't a typical murder scene."

"Okay," she replied meeting Chris' gaze. She took another step toward the threshold and realized that she hadn't brought anything with her to record evidence. She turned to Sgt. Hammond. "Do you have a notepad on you?" she inquired with a sly smile. "I forgot to grab mine."

Sgt. Antonio Hammond was slightly taller than Carmen which made him about 5'9". He had been fortunate to inherit good genes from both his mother and father. His golden brown skin and thick black hair were gifts from the Spanish ancestry on his mother's side. His soulful green eyes, sculpted chin, and impressive stature were a few of the traits he could thank his father for, a well-known wide receiver from Nebraska.

Sgt. Hammond reached into his uniform pocket and handed Carmen a notebook and pen. A faint smile curled up at the ends of his mouth. "Don't worry about returning it," he assured. "I have another one in my car."

At a crime scene, it was known among the officers that Carmen wrote down every significant and seemingly insignificant fact. She would start with a sketch of the scene; take measurements; note the date and time; jot down what the weather was like; if lights were on or off; etc. Every page of Sgt. Hammond's pocketsize notebook would be used. More often than not, these minute details had helped glue a case together. If for some reason they had been overlooked, the investigation could have easily been buried in the cold case files.

Carmen noticed immediately that there had been no forced entry as she stepped into the apartment. There were no pry marks or wood splintering along the doorframe. The solid oak front door showed no evidence of damage either.

There were no visual signs of tampering with the deadbolt or the doorknob itself.

She moved past the entryway and observed a neatly arranged living room to her right. There were two black leather recliners and a square, black lacquer end table. A big screen television was in the far corner with a vase of long stemmed red roses sitting on top of it. An exercise bike was pushed against the far wall with a fuzzy brown teddy bear sitting on the seat.

Out of the corner of her left eye, Carmen caught a glimpse of a scene that made her skin crawl and goose bumps explode onto her arms. She turned slowly and instantly felt her dinner rapidly climbing up her throat. Swallowing hard, she murmured, "Oh, God."

Like the first glimpse of a small coastal town that had been destroyed by a hurricane, the crime scene was overwhelming. It appeared as if someone had sprayed red paint in strange patterns all over the dining room. Little red droplets streamed down the walls forming tiny puddles on the glossy white ceramic floor. The multicolored stained glass lamp that hung above the dining room table was dripping with the same red substance. It didn't take a rocket scientist to figure out what the substance was or to whom it belonged. Lying on the table was a slender, white female in her early twenties.

The victim's blood soaked hair made it difficult to tell the exact color, but possibly light brown or blond. Her eyelids had been taped open with masking tape leaving the lifeless smoky gray eyes staring helplessly at the ceiling. Furthermore, the young woman had been eviscerated, meaning she had been slit from the pelvic bone to the breastbone exposing the inner organs. Her vaginal area had multiple stab wounds, but she had no facial abrasions or defense wounds on her hands indicating a struggle. Her ears were double-pierced and a small rose tattoo was barely distinguishable on her right breast. Her long slender fingers had a coat of sparkling pink polish on the nails. A knife had been deliberately placed in the victim's left hand and a folded up piece of paper in her right.

Carmen was startled by a sudden flash and jumped in spite of herself. "Sorry about that," the crime scene photographer, Debra Sterling, apologized.

"That's okay," Carmen replied, having been so absorbed in her note taking and with the theory she was working on that she hadn't noticed the arrival of the crime scene team.

Carmen moved gingerly around the table watching every step and breathing in with every detail. She scribbled feverishly. She noted that none of the victim's fingernails was missing. The clothes that the victim had apparently been wearing at the time of the attack were neatly folded and placed on the imitation marble countertop in the adjacent kitchen without a drop of blood on them. There was no bruising around the women's ankles or wrists indicating that she had not been restrained. In fact, the victim's hands and feet had been purposely wiped clean of any blood, but why?

"Detective Moore?" a voice whispered. "Detective Moore, are you okay?"

Carmen barely heard the coroner, Mike Sexton, say her name for the second time. She shifted her deep hazel eyes to his and offered an acknowledging nod. Words eluded her for the moment as her mind raced to find answers to questions that quite possibly might never be solved. Who could have committed such a horrific crime? How much time had passed since this poor girl had moved on to a better place? Did anyone hear anything? Was she going though a bad break up? Was she just a random victim selected for convenience?

"Hello, Mike," Carmen finally acknowledged without faltering, though her stomach felt like it had been turned into dough and twisted into the shape of a pretzel. "Give me just a second; I need to talk to Chris about a couple of things."

"Take your time," Mike responded slipping on a pair of latex gloves.

She moved past the coroner and stepped into the kitchen. Chris had just finished examining the drawers and cabinets in the kitchen. "So, what do you have?" she pressed.

"Well, this is what we know so far," Chris began. "Dispatch received a call about 11:25 p.m. Initially, the dispatcher thought the call might be a prank."

"Why?"

"At first, the dispatcher reported that she couldn't even understand what the caller was saying because he was breathing so hard into the phone. She thought it might be an obscene phone call from one of the homeless people that drift through this area looking for food and shelter. So, she told the caller to either report a crime or get off the line. After a couple of seconds had passed without a response, the dispatcher started to hang up. But, just as she began to remove the receiver from her ear, a rough voice on the other end of the line bellowed that we would find a 'lovely corpse' at this address."

"That's nice," Carmen replied sarcastically.

"I had the dispatcher pull the tape with the recorded conversation on it and log it into evidence."

"Smart thinking," Carmen complimented. "Did dispatch have a number come up on the caller I.D.?"

"Yes," Chris affirmed. "The call came from the pay phone that is directly across the street from here. I have an officer over there right now with one of the crime scene guys."

"Anything else I should know?"

"It doesn't appear that the victim is missing any cutlery," he said with a shrug.

"So, the killer brought the knife with him to kill his victim and left it behind for us to find?" Carmen speculated thoughtfully.

"It appears that way." Chris replied.

"Interesting," Carmen remarked.

"What's your take on the victim?"

"She's been dead for a few hours," Carmen informed. "Rigor mortis is already starting to set in."

"That means the caller was more than likely the killer," Chris reasoned aloud.

"Probably," Carmen agreed. "Most of the blood hasn't even had time to completely dry yet. And, who in their right mind would call a police station about a 'lovely' corpse?"

"No one I know," Chris smirked.

"Well, that's a relief," Carmen said with a wink. "I'll see what, if anything, Mike can tell us about the victim." Carmen walked back over to where Mike was recording his primary findings about the victim on audiotape.

Mike was as tall as he was round and incredibly intelligent. His dark brown hair was receding and his once perfect 20/20 vision had faded causing him to wear black-rimmed bifocals. He had been the coroner for over ten years, but he and Carmen had only known one another for about three. Through the course of endless investigations, they had become good friends. She trusted his findings and he welcomed her ideas and insight about cases.

"So, what do you think?" Carmen prompted.

"Ah, Detective Moore, the question is what do you think?" he challenged.

"I think she might have been strangled to death and then stabbed. I don't know why and I sure can't tell with all the blood, but there is something meticulous about all this," she replied pushing the sleeves of her sweatshirt up to her elbows.

"Go on," Mike encouraged.

"As of right now, no one saw anything or heard any screaming. I know my neighbors would have called my apartment if they had suspected any foul play going on in here. Plus, the victim appears to have no defense wounds from a knife attack and this is the only room with a drop of blood in it. I think this girl had already passed on to greener pastures way before this maniac's butchering began."

"Is that all?" Mike pressed, crossing his arms and raising his left hand so that his index finger tapped gently on his lips as the rest of his fingers cradle his chin.

"Well, the killer obviously wiped the blood from the victim's wrists and ankles. He or she also made sure we would notice the rose tattoo on her breast. It's almost like he wanted to be sure that we knew he was in control the whole time."

Mike couldn't resist smiling. He absolutely adored Carmen's ability to logically think of the illogical and make it seem sensible. He had been one of the few to witness the many hours that Carmen spent going over autopsy reports, crime scene photos, testimonials, and her personal notes about a case. She worked exceptionally hard and invested her whole heart into solving a crime. Maybe that was the reason her superiors respected her so much and her fellow officers would go to great lengths to help her. She had a passion for solving cases that seemed to have been etched into her soul.

"I'll perform the autopsy as soon as we get this precious thing identified. I'll page you when I've completed my report. Now, go back to bed and let the crime scene team do their job," Mike insisted in a fatherly tone. "Your eyes are swollen and there are dark circles forming underneath them. You look like hell and you know it won't be long before the nightly news crews swarm upon us like flies on left out watermelon. Imagine the damage to your dating prospects."

"You're funny," Carmen replied sarcastically, amused by his wit. "I'll see you tomorrow."

"It is tomorrow," he reminded.

She gave him a genuine smile before walking back over to Chris who was patiently waiting for her at the door. "Do we know who the victim is yet?" she questioned, stifling a yawn.

"Well, it's probably going to be Marie Sutton, the girl who is the sole occupant of this apartment," Chris informed. "But, we won't be 100% sure until her mother comes down to make a positive I.D. We're sending an officer over there now to pick her up."

"Make sure the officer gives the crime lab time to process the victim and Mike time to clean her up a little bit," Carmen urged. "No mother deserves seeing her daughter like that."

"I will," Chris agreed. "Why don't you call it a night and get some rest. If we find any evidence worthy of waking you, I'll be the first one pounding on your door."

"Alright, Chris," Carmen agreed reluctantly. "But, let me know if…"

"What's wrong?" Chris prodded in response to Carmen's abrupt silence.

"It completely slipped my mind," she blurted out, spinning around on her heels.

Chris followed Carmen over to the victim where she borrowed a pair of latex gloves from one of the crime scene guys. She slipped her hands into the gloves and carefully removed the folded piece of paper from the victim's right hand. She unfolded it and read the words written in bold, black lettering.

"What does it say?" Chris urged.

The room fell eerily silent. Carmen tried to control the anger surging through her like an electrical current. She read it aloud through gritted teeth:

"So easy, so soft, and so much fun...I moved
so fast, she had no time to run."

Carmen refolded the piece of paper and placed it into an evidence bag. She handed the bag to one of the crime scene technicians to label and followed Chris out of the apartment. "Call me if you find anything," she insisted.

"You have my word," Chris assured.

"I know," Carmen stated, pushing open the stairwell door.

"You know, you can stay at our place tonight if you want," Chris suggested, trying not to sound too concerned. "You can even bring that Chihuahua of yours."

Touched by his kindness, Carmen squeezed his hand and chuckled, "I'll be just fine. Besides, people will think we're in love and do you know what that will do for my reputation? I'd probably never get another date."

"I had to at least try to get you to walk on the wild side for once," he teased.

"I do walk on the wild side," Carmen reminded with an ornery grin.

"All joking aside," Chris said, shoving his hands deep into his pants pockets. "Call me if you need me, okay?"

Carmen gave him an appreciative smile and headed up to her apartment without looking back. Sweat began to bead on her forehead before she realized she was running up the dimly lit steps. She threw both hands on the long silver handle of the seventh floor stairwell door and it sprang open. She fumbled with her keys as she approached her apartment. She slid the key into the doorknob and unlocked it. Cuffs' recognizable bark greeted her from behind the closed door. She quickly opened it and stepped inside.

CHAPTER TWO

With her heart pounding against her chest like thunderous rain on a sidewalk, Carmen quickly secured the deadbolt and latched the security chain. Cuffs jumped excitedly at her feet yearning to be picked up, but she purposely ignored him. She removed the Glock 40 from the holster and double-checked every room, closet, and other hiding space a knife-wielding lunatic might hide. Satisfied that she was alone, she re-holstered the Glock and scooped Cuffs up into her arms.

Cuffs was a golden brown Chihuahua that closely resembled a baby deer. He had dark chocolate colored eyes and a patch of snowy white hair underneath his chin. The very tip of his slender tail appeared to have been dipped in black paint. Even though he wasn't big enough to harm an intruder, he was an excellent watchdog. His keen sense of hearing enabled him to alert Carmen to approaching visitors whether good or bad.

Carmen had been blessed by his unexpected arrival as a birthday present a few years earlier. The moment she saw him, she fell in love. Since then, she rarely went anywhere without him except for work. She had moved into her present home, one of the two spacious apartments on the seventh floor, so that Cuffs had more space to run.

Her living room was approximately 600 square feet and contained a beautiful light brown and beige couch that encircled a black glass coffee table with a gold Panther engraved on it. There were neither police magazines nor expensive trinkets cluttering it up. The remote to the television and two handheld video game controllers were the only things Carmen kept on it. One of the newest game systems on the market was hooked up to the 42-inch flat screen television directly in front of the couch and some games were stacked neatly beside the entertainment stand. On the bookshelf to the left of the television, there were Star Wars and Coca-Cola collectibles that included action figures, bottles, and battleships.

The kitchen was quite large compared to the one Carmen's mom had when she was growing up. The tile floor was an intricate design of white and peacock blue specks. The white countertops were also splashed with the same blue color. The island had a built-in gas range with a grilling station on one end and a sturdy counter inlaid with a cutting board on the other. Carmen could fix an entire Thanksgiving dinner and never worry about running out of space to cook.

A few feet away from the kitchen was her home office. It contained a teak desk with a swivel black leather chair. A computer, scanner, and fax machine were strategically placed on top of it and were networked to her computer at work. Above the desk there were quite a few plaques honoring her accomplishments in police work. A small bookcase with a complete set of encyclopedias and various titles of lesbian fiction by her favorite authors was nestled in one corner. A workout bench and stair stepper occupied the other corner.

The other two remaining rooms were the bedroom and bathroom. A queen-size sleigh bed was nestled between the balcony window and walk-in closet. An old chest of

drawers with strips of paint missing from the bottom edges
was pushed against the back wall and a net full of stuffed
animals hung down from the ceiling beside it. The bathroom
was accessible from the bedroom as well as the hallway. The
tub had Jacuzzi-like jets in it, though Carmen rarely had time
to use it because of her hectic schedule. The sink had been
designed to resemble a sand dollar and the faucets were gold-
plated.

This laid-back appearance of Carmen's home amused
most people who came to visit. It didn't seem to fit a serious-
minded detective at all and that's what she loved about it.
Her home was her salvation from the daily encounters with
horrific crimes and heart-broken families. When she played
video games it took her mind to a different dimension where
if she didn't win, it didn't matter. She could always restart the
game, unlike detective work where that wasn't an option.
And, when she wanted to beat to death the bastard who raped
an innocent fifteen-year old girl, she could bench press her
way out of the darkness of hatred and refocus on the
guidance of evidence. This was her haven from the violence-
plagued world in which she spent day after day in.

Carmen set Cuffs on the couch and slipped off her
shoes. She switched on her CD player and the music of
Kenny G. filled the air. She glanced at the digital clock on the
microwave and noticed it was 3:36 a.m., a chilling 4 hours
since she had been alerted to the tragedy on the first floor.
She laid her head down on one of the cushy sofa pillows and
stretched out her legs. Cuffs waited a mere two seconds
before making his move. He nestled himself between the
couch cushions and Carmen's right side before laying his head
on her breast. His warm little body stirred as she gently
rubbed his ears.

At 11:21 a.m., Carmen was awakened by her pager
vibrating itself right off the edge of the coffee table. Cuffs ran

up to it, barking as if it were a burglar breaking in to steal his bone. He cocked his head to one side and grabbed the belt clip between his teeth shaking the pager violently. Carmen reached down and patted him on the head, "What a ferocious dog you are! Now, release it." Cuffs dropped the pager and looked up at her with his tail wagging feverishly.

She looked at the pager's display and instantly recognized Mike's work number. She hurried into the bathroom and studied her reflection. Her eyes were bloodshot, there were indentations from the couch pillow lining her left cheek, and the sickening smells of last night's crime scene seemed to have taken refuge in her nostrils. Of course, there was her hair to take into account and no amount of brushing would resolve that craziness. It truly looked like she had stuck her head out the window of a racecar barreling around a track and doused her hair with hairspray.

"I have to shower," she declared stripping off her clothes.

After showering, Carmen slipped on a pair of navy blue dress slacks and a thin, short-sleeve, silk dress shirt. She pulled her baby fine, blond hair back into a ponytail before moving into the bedroom to grab her freshly charged cell phone from the dresser. She selected Chris' number from the recent call list and pressed the green 'send' button.

"This is Detective Duhn."

"Hey, it's me."

"Hey Carmen," Chris greeted. "What's up?"

"I didn't wake you, did I?"

"Nah, I've been up for a couple of hours."

"You didn't sleep at all, did you?"

"No," Chris admitted. "There was a lot of evidence to process. I just came home to change my clothes and have breakfast with Mary."

"Well, Mike just paged me," Carmen informed. "I'll see what he has to say and then meet you at the station in an hour or so."

"Sounds good," Chris replied. "See you later."

Carmen flipped her phone closed and went into the kitchen to make sure Cuffs had enough food and water. She knew that it was going to be a very long day. And, although Cuffs was completely potty trained to go in the litter box that was strategically hidden in the living room, she enjoyed their morning walks together. "I'll be back in a little while and then we can go to the park," she assured him.

Cuffs began leaping at her legs and barking playfully. She always hated to leave him, especially if she hadn't had time to give him his much-deserved affection. He would just sit down beside the door and look up at her with his big, sappy, brown eyes. Sometimes, he would even throw in the extra touch of whimpering at her. Now, as she grabbed her badge and radio, he was at her feet. "I'm sorry, buddy, but you have to stay here," she said opening the front door. Cuffs stayed as instructed, but he peered out at her pitifully. Carmen felt as though she were abandoning a child as she closed the door and secured the deadbolt.

Carmen stood motionless outside her front door contemplating her next move. She wasn't too thrilled with the options before her. She could take the elevator but there was always a chance of getting stuck for hours or the cables snapping from excessive use. Of course, maybe that option didn't seem favorable because it exploited her fear of falling. On the other hand, the door that led to the stairwell seemed uninviting. The frigidness of the air escaping from beneath the one-inch space below the door chilled her to the bone.

In disgust, she walked over to the elevator and pressed the 'down' button. She listened as it painfully made its ascent to the seventh floor. The buzzer sounded and the elevator doors parted. She pressed the button for the first level and paced back and forth nervously. She tried to occupy her mind by mentally reviewing the facts she knew so far about the murder.

The elevator arrived on the first floor and Carmen stepped out as soon as the doors opened. She peered down the hallway toward apartment #5. The crime scene was still cordoned off and a day-shift officer was guarding the entrance. She greeted him with a wave and he gave her an acknowledging nod. She walked toward the solid steel door knowing that she and Chris would return later in the day to take another look. She pushed the door open and shielded her eyes from the sun's unrelenting rays that bombarded her. As she left the sanctity of her apartment complex, the smell of rotting trash oozing out of the dumpsters in the back lot urged her to hold her breath until she reached her car.

She slipped behind the wheel of her 2004 red Corvette and started the engine. The mid-August sun had turned it into a mobile sauna. The driver's seat was scorching and she could barely touch the steering wheel without burning the palms of her hands. Little drops of sweat began to form on the back of her neck underneath her ponytail and across her brow.

• • •

Carmen whipped into the parking lot behind the coroner's office just as the air conditioner finally decided to start spitting out cold air. She continued past the visitor parking into the reserved lot and searched for an empty spot amongst the police cruisers and other city-owned vehicles. Out of the corner of her eye, Carmen noticed a dark blue Blazer pulling into a front row parking space. She accidentally hit the brakes with childlike excitement and the tread of the tires gripped the asphalt instantly. The smell of hot rubber spewed into the air.

Carmen quickly lifted her foot off the brake and proceeded toward the front row. She eased her car into a parking space about six spaces down from where the Blazer had just parked. She turned off the engine and opened the glove compartment quickly pulling everything out of it. She pretended to arrange the contents as she peered through the side window at the woman sitting behind the steering wheel of the Blazer. She hoped the three cars between them camouflaged her real intentions sufficiently.

• • •

Zoë Childers opened the driver's side door and stepped into the Florida sunshine. She was 5'9 with dark brown hair, sparkling emerald eyes, and a deep, rich tan. Her sculpted physique would make almost anyone quiver with desire. She was exceptionally intelligent as well, having attained degrees in both criminal justice and forensic psychology. She specialized in cases involving serial killers and had just finished solving a string of prostitute killings.

Although highly respected, most people knew very little about Zoë. She was rarely seen out on the town and always seemed to be on duty. Carmen wondered if her subtle indifference to everyone was all just an act to keep her personal and professional lives as separate as possible. Still, no one could deny that Zoë had the ability to bring out the best in people whenever she was around.

• • •

Zoë noticed the red Corvette that had whipped into the parking lot. She knew exactly to whom it belonged. She tried to maintain her composure as she locked the doors of the Blazer with the remote and casually walked toward the space where the corvette had parked. She found the driver to be extremely sexy, but inevitably became tongue-tied on matters that weren't professional in nature.

Carmen waited until Zoë was in front of the corvette to close the glove compartment. She loved Zoë's casual style of dress, especially when she wore the loose fitting pair of faded blue jeans that she had on today. She also enjoyed the variety of cop shirts that Zoë seemed to have an abundance of. Today Zoë's t-shirt read "just hafta fight crime" and it complimented her wide shoulders and strong back exquisitely. Carmen restrained her lips from turning into a big goofy grin as she opened the car door. "Hi, Detective Childers," she greeted.

"Well, Detective Moore, do I have you to thank for the cancellation of my day off?" Zoë remarked as Carmen stepped out and closed the door. "If I do, I know who will be buying my lunch today."

Carmen loved the way Zoë talked to her, especially since she had never known her to talk to anyone else in the same demeanor. She wondered if Zoë's charismatic charm was the same under more personal circumstances. And, what if it was? Would she feel this nervous? Her cool, calm, collective self always faded whenever Zoë came around.

Carmen blushed as she realized that her eyes had just traveled up and down the length of Zoë's body. "Oh God, did she notice that?" she thought, slightly panicked. Unable to look Zoë in the eyes, Carmen focused on answering her question, "I don't think I'm responsible. I'm just here to talk to Mike about a murder that happened last night."

"Well, it seems that Mike called my Captain and informed him that my presence would be greatly appreciated as well," Zoë replied, tensing every muscle in her body just in case Carmen decided to take another look.

Surprised and somewhat taken off guard, Carmen looked slightly insulted, "When did they call you?"

Zoë understood how upsetting it could be when another detective was called in to assist on a case without the approval of the lead investigator. "Just a little bit ago," she revealed uneasily. "Captain said that my insane passion with serial killers might be useful on this case."

"Well then, I should be the first to welcome you to the case," Carmen stated attempting to diffuse her defensiveness as they walked along the sidewalk toward the coroner's office. "Especially since it occurred at my apartment complex last night."

A concerned expression developed on Zoë's face, "Your building?"

"Yeah, late last night, and it was pretty bad. I guess I should have known Mike would suggest calling someone in with your expertise," Carmen stated thoughtfully. "And, I'm glad you're the one they chose."

"Me too," Zoë admitted, opening the front door that led into the coroner's office for Carmen. "By the way, you look really nice today."

"Thank you," Carmen managed through her utter shock. "You look really nice too."

"I haven't seen you in a while," Zoë said, placing her hand on Carmen's shoulder. "Anything new?"

Carmen turned around and smiled, "Not really. What about you?"

"Nah, just working."

Carmen could sense that Zoë had something weighing on her mind and not knowing what it might be was killing her. "Are you alright?" she prodded.

"You should be extra careful," Zoë replied, unable to maintain eye contact.

"I will. I promise," Carmen assured. "Are you worried about little ol' me?"

"Just a little," Zoë answered.

As their eyes met, there was no mistaking the truth revealed in each other's gaze. The desire to be in each other's arms evaporated the two feet of distance between them. Carmen tilted her head upward and Zoë's body visibly trembled as she leaned into Carmen. Carmen felt her heart lift from the realms of solitude as Zoë's hands grasped her shoulders and pulled her even closer. Carmen closed her eyes and could feel Zoë's breath against her lips.

"Are you two ever going to get in here?" Mike snickered, striding into the entryway and causing Zoë and Carmen to jump away from each other.

Mike had secretly been a confidant for both women for years. They each had come to him to inquire about the other. He had relentlessly tried to persuade both of them to ask the other out, but to no avail. Now, he grasped every opportunity that he could find to get the two of them to work on a case together.

"We were just on our way in," Carmen stammered.

"The way the two of you were looking at each other gave me the inkling that work was not the main priority at that moment," he said, trying to keep a straight face.

"We were just talking," Zoë claimed, her voice drenched in guilt.

"That would require your mouths actually moving," Mike replied good-naturedly. "Anyway, I've discovered a few things that will interest both of you."

"Well, I guess we better get going," Zoë managed, finding it difficult to speak.

"Yeah, I guess we should," Carmen agreed trying to maintain a professional tone. "You go ahead. I'll be there in just a second."

"Are you okay?" Zoë questioned nervously.

"I'm fine," Carmen assured with a genuine smile. "Just need to use the restroom."

"Okay."

Carmen walked toward the restrooms that were located on the opposite end of the building as Zoë strutted after Mike. Carmen's imagination savored a brief vision of Zoë's long, sensuous legs being wrapped around her in a moment of passion. Desire stole the moisture from her mouth and transported it to the small valley between her legs. She took a few more steps forward and felt as though the whole room was spinning. She closed her eyes to refocus and tried to hide the smile that touched her lips. But, it was useless. Her heart refused to be caged and it fluttered stubbornly causing her smile to broaden with every step.

• • •

Carmen felt momentarily disoriented as the door clicked shut behind her. The autopsy room always reeked of a musty odor that grabbed hold of her sense of smell with talons of steel. She instantly began breathing through her mouth. Her eyes narrowed, her smile faded, and her body broke out into a mild case of goose bumps that faded almost as quickly as they appeared. She squared her shoulders and walked very purposely toward where Zoë and Mike were conversing. The sounds of her footsteps bounced off the floor and reverberated off the light gray concrete walls.

Carmen did not look forward to her occasional visits to this place. But, her passion to catch the ones responsible for taking the life of an innocent person required her to be there. In fact, it was what pulled her across the room to the autopsy table time after time. And, it was what pulled her now. She peered down at the victim with her heart hidden underneath her sleeve and the 'tough as nails' image riding above it.

Carmen despised how the slick, metallic, oblong table where the poor victim's naked body rested seemed not to cradle her innocence, but betray it with cold, uncaring reminders of the bleakness of the world. She cleared her throat, "Well, I know you didn't call Zoë and me down here for nothing, so what did you find?"

Tugging at the collar of his pure white lab coat, Mike gave her a half-cocked smile, "You were right on the money about this victim."

Zoë looked bewildered, "She was right about what?"

"Carmen thought that the victim might have been strangled," Mike informed. "And, in fact, she was. Her windpipe was crushed and the discoloration around her neck is due to bruising caused by the suspect. I believe we're looking for a male intruder."

"Go on," Zoë urged.

"The imprints around her neck are very large and the damage was extensive. The blood vessels in her eyes ruptured due to the force of strangulation. She probably lost consciousness in less than five seconds from lack of oxygen to the brain. Fortunately for her, she was already dead when the killer started cutting her up."

"So, I suppose Zoë was called in on this case because of the mutilation to the body?" Carmen prodded.

"Exactly," Mike confirmed. "If you can humor me for a few minutes, I'll explain." Both Carmen and Zoë remained silent as Mike bent over the body. "Right here," he began pointing to a crude cut along the victim's stomach, "something or someone startled the killer. It's highly probable that someone came in the front door of the apartment building and spooked him."

"People come in and out of that building all the time," Carmen stated. "Wouldn't he be expecting that?"

"Just hear me out, okay?" Not waiting for a response, Mike continued, "The killer would have had an almost perfectly straight line from pelvic bone to breastbone. But, he jerked the knife to the right and then removed it. It seems to me, that whatever startled him also caused him to believe that he might be interrupted."

"Could someone else have been in the room?" Zoë inquired.

"The two of you are so impatient," Mike said as he pointed to the victim's vaginal area. "These marks were made with the same precision, but they're in a pattern or something."

"Were they made before or after her death?" Zoë questioned.

"They were made after her death as well," Mike replied.

"If that's true, how did the room get covered in so much blood?" Zoë demanded.

"He staged it to look that way," Carmen answered flatly. "He wanted us to believe this was a frenzied attack, not a cold calculated one."

"Exactly," Mike agreed. "And to answer your earlier question, I don't believe that there was anyone else in the room. This was definitely the work of one individual."

"How can you tell?" Carmen quizzed.

"The angle and depth of the wounds are identical," Mike informed.

"Is our guy left-handed?" Carmen hoped.

"No," Mike retorted. "He's definitely right-handed."

"At least when wielding a knife," Zoë interjected. "I know plenty of people who write left-handed but do everything else with their right hand."

"True," Mike ceded.

"Have you determined an approximate time of death?" Carmen asked, taking a closer look at the multiple stab wounds in the vaginal area.

"Well, I would say between 8 p.m. and 11 p.m. But, after talking to Chris a few minutes ago, I'm betting closer to 8:45 p.m."

Carmen stared at Mike with child-like anticipation, "Why do you think it was closer to 8:45 p.m.?"

"Well, Chris said that all of the residents but one stayed home after eight o'clock." Looking at his notebook, Mike continued, "Ms. Ann Johnston, who works nights, informed Chris that she left her apartment about 8:45 p.m. She remembered the time because she had checked it after slamming her front door closed in order for the deadbolt to line up with the lock properly. She's been having trouble with it for the past few days and prayed that no one was sleeping. Then, she reported that she talked to you, Carmen."

Surprised that she had forgotten that encounter and dreading where this admission may lead, Carmen nodded, "She did talk to me. I had just finished walking Cuffs and I was coming up the steps outside our apartment complex when she stepped outside. We chatted for a few minutes and then I got my mail and went up to my apartment."

Zoë had been listening intensely and her face became flushed. Eyeing Mike, she tried to control the quiver of disbelief in her voice, "I hear what you're saying, but I don't believe it. You're theorizing that Ms. Johnston slamming her front door could have been what startled the killer."

"Yes. I believe that might be the case," Mike confirmed.

"And, you're also thinking that the reason he removed the knife from this girl's chest is because he knew it was Carmen that she had ran into outside," Zoë concluded glancing over at Carmen.

"Yes."

"It seems feasible," Carmen interjected. "But, the one thing I don't understand is why he would remove the knife. The victim wasn't screaming, so why would he be concerned about anyone outside? And why would I frighten him? I was just another tenant coming home getting my mail," she reminded, looking back and forth between them.

Mike and Zoë looked at each other with a quiet understanding. Mike touched Carmen's hand, "That's just my theory and I could be way off base. I just thought it was an interesting coincidence to point out."

Carmen analyzed his last statement carefully. She knew full well what he was implying. But, was it feasible to believe that the killer had stalked the victim to the point that he knew that a cop lived in her building? If he did know that, how long had he been watching the victim? Did he remove the knife from that girl's chest cavity just in case that inquisitive cop knocked on the door?

"Can I have a pen and paper?" Zoë asked, interrupting Carmen's thoughts. "I know this sounds crazy, but these stab wounds look more deliberate."

"What do you mean?" Carmen pressed.

"If you look at it just right, it seems to spell out a word," Zoë informed. "I think it's the word 'more'."

"You know, I have to agree with you. I thought the pattern was unusual, but I never imagined it spelled out a word," Mike exclaimed, impressed by Zoë's findings. "Good job!"

"So, what do you think it means?" Carmen inquired taking a closer look.

"Well, it could mean a couple of things," Zoë answered. "It could mean that there are more victims that we haven't found yet. Or, it could mean that this victim was just the start."

"Great," Carmen sighed disheartened.

"I'll try to come up with a preliminary profile. There isn't a lot to go on at the moment, but he's probably a white male and has an inferiority complex toward women." Taking a closer look at the victim's wounds, Zoë continued, "And, this isn't the first time he's killed someone."

Both Mike and Carmen stared at her. Finally, Carmen breathed more of the question than spoke it, "What?"

"The killer planned, executed, and completed this sick fantasy with a call to the police," Zoë elaborated. "The murderer is perfecting his skill. I'd bet my badge that he has already chosen his next victim."

CHAPTER THREE

Carmen and Zoë walked out of the coroner's office in awkward silence and headed toward the parking lot. Their purposeful gait slowed as they neared Zoë's Blazer. Carmen was desperate not to allow the moment to pass by for the umpteenth time. She took a deep breath of the steaming hot Florida air, "I absolutely hate how dirty I feel after I leave that room."

Zoë looked at her amused, "I know what you mean. All I want to do is strip my clothes off and take a nice hot shower."

"Me too," Carmen agreed, enjoying that thought and squinting against the radiant sun in a cloudless blue sky to gaze into Zoë's eyes.

"Are you headed back to the station?"

"Yeah," Carmen replied praying for anything resembling a flirtatious gesture. Even a cheesy pickup line would be alright with her. "What about you?"

"I'm going to run home and change," Zoë said moving over to the driver's side door of the Blazer. "I don't think my attire would really go over well with your captain. I heard he's a stickler."

"Well, that's definitely true, but I think you look great," Carmen blurted out before she could stop herself.

"Thanks." Zoë replied easily.

"I guess I'll see you later then," Carmen stated, her cheeks reddening. She scolded herself silently for the blatant honesty.

Zoë opened her car door and closed it without getting in. She paused for a brief moment before stepping back over to where Carmen was standing on the sidewalk. She felt as though her stomach had transformed into an active volcano, but instead of ash, it spewed millions of teeny butterflies fluttering with nervous energy. Expecting a rejection, she swallowed hard; "Do you want to grab a bite to eat around lunch time?"

"I'm not sure if I can get away," Carmen replied her heart crashing against the rocks of professional responsibility.

"That's okay," Zoë remarked with a dismissive wave feeling the color drain from her face.

"Maybe we could get together around six tonight instead?" Carmen suggested bravely. "You could swing by my apartment or vice versa. We could grab a bite to eat and maybe even catch a movie."

"Sure," Zoë agreed. "I'll be over at six o'clock sharp."

• • •

Carmen dashed into her apartment causing Cuffs to run for his life. He dove underneath the soft cotton blanket in his little dog bed. "Cuffs, I am so sorry!" she shouted from the bedroom. "I was so caught up in this case that time slipped away from me."

She laughed at the thought of someone listening in on her conversations with Cuffs. Surely, they would wonder if all homicide detectives chose canine companions over human ones. However, she truly considered Cuffs to be her best friend. He had been the most faithful companion compared to all the other people that had managed to cross her path. It pained her sometimes to know that dogs had better morals than most people did.

"And, my little man, I think I have a date tonight!" she cooed. "Guess who it's with?" Cuffs looked up at her as she rounded the couch and walked over to where he was still partially hidden underneath the blanket. "It's with Zoë Childers," she declared excitedly. "Can you believe it?"

She reached down and patted him on the head. He wagged his tail before rolling onto his side and offering his belly. She glanced at the wall clock above the television and knew Zoë would be knocking on the door in a half-hour. She gave his belly a few gentle scratches before heading to the bathroom.

She took an extra couple of minutes in the shower to shave her legs and underarms although she was sure no one would benefit from her smoothness but herself. Her strong moral upbringing resulted in her extreme selectiveness of whom she allowed into her bed. And though she had allowed herself to be insanely stupid and drink way too much for about six months when she was in her early twenties, she only wanted to share her bed, her body, and her heart with someone she truly loved.

She finished drying off, hurried over to the walk-in closet, and began rummaging through her clothes for the perfect outfit. She couldn't stop thinking about what Zoë might be wearing. Of course, she couldn't resist thinking about what she might not be wearing later on down the road if everything went well tonight. After a few more minutes of searching, she settled on a flattering baby blue sweater and a pair of nicely fitting blue jeans.

She finished applying the last bit of eyeliner underneath her left eye just as Cuffs began barking. She double-checked her makeup in the mirror before switching off the bathroom light. She walked into the front room and took a deep breath trying to calm the nerves rattling throughout her body. A soft knock resonated from the front door. Cuffs tore across the living room and gave his best guard dog performance filled with ferocious barks.

Carmen walked over to the door and glanced down at what she was wearing one last time. She noticed that her enthusiasm reflected in her breasts. "Great," she thought reaching for the doorknob slightly embarrassed. She opened the door and felt her already hardened nipples ache to be grasped by the hands of the beautiful woman standing in the doorway. "Hi," she greeted trying to keep her eyes from traveling up and down Zoë's body once again.

Zoë wore a very flattering pair of dark blue jeans and a silky white button-up shirt. Her golden tan could be seen discreetly through her shirt as well as the white lacy bra she was wearing. Her shoulder length dark brown hair fell softly around her face. Carmen could smell the subtle, sweet scent of her perfume wafting in the air. And, she noticed that in Zoë's left hand, she had what appeared to be a small bone.

Zoë smiled warmly at Carmen before dropping down to one knee. She gave the bone to Cuffs, who was curiously peeking into the hallway. Scratching his back, she began to introduce herself, "It is very nice to meet you, Cuffs. I'm Zoë. Your mom and I are working on a case together, so you don't have to concern yourself with biting me, you fearless thing."

Carmen was impressed by this thoughtful action. She remembered mentioning Cuffs only one time with Zoë present and that had been a few months back. Now, here she was bringing Cuffs a dog bone and talking to him like a little person. This woman definitely knew how to get to her.

"Are you ready to go?" Zoë asked standing back up and not assuming Carmen was going to invite her in.

"Sure," Carmen replied. She pulled the door closed with Cuffs safe inside and secured the deadbolt.

Zoë pushed the button for the elevator as soon as Carmen was at her side. When the elevator doors opened a minute or so later, Carmen realized that she still had not said anything. It was uncharacteristic of her to feel so shy and vulnerable. She was attracted to Zoë but not merely because of her looks, although that was a bonus. She was mostly smitten with the uncanny way that Zoë brought out the woman in her that she had forbid anyone in the past to see.

"I'm sorry if I'm not very talkative," Carmen began as they stepped onto the elevator. "I've been so busy with this new case today that I haven't had a chance to unwind yet."

Zoë smiled; "That's okay. I spent most of the day getting up to speed on what happened last night. I came by earlier and checked out the crime scene. Plus, I wanted to make sure I knew how to get here so I wouldn't be late."

"You're so thoughtful," Carmen complimented, but intrigue clouded her thoughts. "So, did you learn anything from the scene?"

"I found a small dark brown fiber next to one of the table legs," Zoë proclaimed. "It could be part of the same fibers that the crime scene team collected, but I gave it to them anyway."

Carmen heard the hint of disappointment in Zoë's voice. "Let's make a deal," Carmen suggested apologetically. "I don't want either one of us to mention the case tonight. Let's just go out and have some fun. I'm pretty sure we've both earned it."

Zoë gave her a heartfelt smile; "Works for me, I just want to know more about the woman behind the badge."

The elevator arrived on the first floor and Zoë squeezed Carmen's hand tenderly before stepping into the hallway. She was aware of the fact that the night sergeant was posted out in front of apartment #5. Carmen, on the other hand, had allowed her mind to set sail on a fantasy voyage with Zoë at the helm. She stood in the elevator long enough for the doors to begin sliding shut. Instantly, she pushed the button on the control panel that opened the elevator doors and fell in step beside Zoë.

Carmen followed Zoë out the back door and around the complex to Zoë's Blazer. She couldn't help but feel like she was on a date. She was being escorted by an extremely attractive and intelligent woman, whom she had learned years earlier, was a lesbian thanks to Mike. Carmen felt like she was on top of the world and it was a feeling she had long ago forced herself to forget.

• • •

"God, I feel like I'm going to explode," Carmen boasted. "I swear I didn't feel this full when we left the restaurant!"

"Me either," Zoë replied.

Zoë made a hard right turn around a corner and hit the gas before glancing down at the digital clock display. Carmen couldn't help wondering if she had bored Zoë with her rambling. "If you need to take me home, I don't mind," Carmen offered hearing the disappointment in her own voice. "I mean, you seem like you're pressed for time."

Zoë looked at her amused and gently laid her hand on Carmen's knee. "I have a surprise for you and I just want to make sure that we get there on time," she revealed. "I definitely do not want to take you home right now."

"That's good," Carmen admitted. "I really didn't want to go home."

Zoë realized that her hand was still on Carmen's knee. She felt Carmen's body tremble underneath her fingertips. "Oh, God," she thought without moving her hand a single inch. "Please let that be a good sign."

• • •

"Wow, I still can't believe you had tickets for Melissa Etheridge!" Carmen gushed. "What did you do? Sleep with the girl at the ticket counter?"

Zoë laughed; "Now, do you think I'm going to let you know all my secrets on our first night out on the town?"

Zoë had stopped by her sister's house right after she left the coroner's office. She managed to charm her sister out of her ticket by telling her that her whole love life was riding on it. Her sister, Linda, was more than willing to give up the ticket. She knew how long Zoë had been working up the courage to ask Carmen out and she wasn't about to be the one to put a damper on the evening.

"This whole night has been terrific," Carmen said sincerely as they turned onto her street. "Thank you so much!"

"The pleasure was all mine."

Zoë parked the Blazer next to the curb across the street from Carmen's apartment complex. She stepped down out of the driver's seat, walked around to the passenger side, and opened the door for Carmen. She hated the fact that time had gone by so quickly. She wanted to tell Carmen that she wished they could spend more time together, but she didn't want that to be misinterpreted. She'd had too good of a night. She definitely didn't want Carmen to think for one second that she was only interested in sex. If the truth were to be known, she was more interested in obtaining long-term status.

Carmen didn't want the night to end either. She had been scheming to find a way to somehow spend a little bit more time with Zoë. Now, she looked up at Zoë with the most pleading eyes, "Would you mind walking me to my front door? It's a little unnerving with the murder and all."

"Sure, I don't mind," Zoë replied. "I would feel a lot better knowing you were safe and sound inside your apartment anyway."

• • •

Carmen and Zoë stepped off the elevator and walked toward Carmen's front door where they could hear Cuffs barking from inside. Carmen's heart was soaring with the possibility of a kiss. Hadn't they almost kissed earlier at the coroner's office anyway? This would be the perfect opportunity to complete that moment. Besides, she knew if they kissed now that this was an actual date and that Zoë wanted to be more than friends. But if she didn't kiss her, how would she know? What if Zoë was thinking the same thing?

Carmen unlocked the door and partially opened it to let Cuffs know it was her. She turned back around and gazed into Zoë's captivating green eyes. "Thank you again for a wonderful time," she whispered. "I hope we can do something again sometime soon."

Carmen dropped her gaze and bit her bottom lip nervously. She thought that shaking Zoë's hand might be the more appropriate thing to do, but she leaned forward and hugged her instead. Zoë welcomed the hug and wrapped her arms around Carmen squeezing her tightly in return.

"I would very much like to get together again," Zoë whispered. "I really enjoy spending time with you."

Zoë hugged Carmen a little tighter and slowly released her embrace. She wondered if Carmen would really see her again. How could she turn away without telling her that she really cared about her? She wanted to fall down on her knees and beg Carmen to let her into her world. But she wanted Carmen to let her in on her own free will, even if it took forever. "I guess I better let you go," she said reluctantly. "We should probably get some rest before another long day begins."

Carmen knew the moment was passing her by. As Zoë turned to leave, she gathered up her courage and placed her hand softly on Zoë's cheek. She gingerly turned Zoë's face so their lips were only inches apart. She waited for Zoë to resist the advance, but Zoë just stared deeply into her hazel eyes. Carmen slid her hand through Zoë's thick satiny hair and leaned forward. She prayed that Zoë would know what she wanted and would not push her away. Zoë gently pressed her lips to Carmen's.

Their passion flared like a thousand Fourth of July sparklers being ignited all at once. They moved their bodies against one another as though their souls might actually be able to touch if they managed to get close enough. All the feelings that Carmen had suppressed for Zoë yearned to be revealed and it scared her to death. She knew without a doubt that sleeping with Zoë wouldn't just be sex; it would mean a whole lot more.

They inched their way through the opened door and once inside, Carmen pushed the door closed and locked it. She nervously guided Zoë's hand underneath her shirt. Both her and Zoë's breathing quickened as Zoë touched Carmen's soft silky smooth waistline. Zoë ran her fingers around Carmen's sides and up her incredibly toned back. She maneuvered her hands back around to Carmen's stomach and massaged her sides passionately with her fingertips. Carmen realized that Zoë made no attempt whatsoever to touch her breasts indicating how much she respected her.

They made their way into the kitchen. Zoë could see into Carmen's bedroom by the partially opened door. She desperately wanted Carmen, but she didn't want this to be just some one-night stand. She had waited a long time to be invited into Carmen's world. When she felt Carmen squeeze her a little tighter though, her defenses crumbled. Zoë gently slipped her tongue into Carmen's warm, wanting mouth and slid her hands to where they were just beneath Carmen's soft delicate breasts.

Carmen yearned for Zoë to touch. "Please, Zoë," she begged. "I need to feel your touch."

Zoë inched her strong hands up to Carmen's breast. She slipped her fingers underneath the cotton material of Carmen's bra and gently squeezed Carmen's nipples between her fingertips. She enjoyed the silky softness that her hands were cradling. She pulled her lips away from Carmen's only to press them against the right side of her neck. She lingered there for only a moment before she moved her mouth to Carmen's ear and ran her tongue around the outer edge. Then, she flicked her tongue seductively against Carmen's earlobe.

Carmen's hands drifted up the front of Zoë's body. She stopped at the top button of Zoë's shirt and unbuttoned it. She continued unbuttoning her shirt until the last one had been undone. She pulled the shirt apart revealing the white lacy bra that Zoë wore. Then, Carmen proceeded to slip the shirt and each bra strap off of Zoë's shoulder and peel away the satiny material from Zoë's breasts.

Carmen grasped Zoë's breasts and began to massage them. Zoë pulled her mouth away from Carmen's ear and gasped. Carmen brought her lips to Zoë's, their tongues foretelling what they desired to do to one another. As their hips collided and rocked against one another, Carmen felt her insecurities surfacing. She abruptly pulled away. "Oh God, Zoë," she breathed. "I want you, but I think we should slow down."

Taken off guard, Zoë released her immediately. "I'm sorry," she stammered.

Carmen could see that Zoë thought she had done something terribly wrong. Carmen laid her head on Zoë's chest and in a very tender voice tried to explain. "You don't have to be sorry," she began softly. "I want to be close to you. I just want you to know me, the real me, not the one everyone else sees."

"I'm not trying to get you into bed," Zoë exclaimed. "I do want to know you and I can wait forever for anything more."

It took all the willpower Zoë had to release her embrace. She knew she was falling for Carmen, but she wanted to make sure that when they did make love, Carmen knew it was love and not just sex. She avoided Carmen's eyes and began buttoning up her shirt. A loud beeping sound filled the air and she glanced down at her pager, "Do you mind if I use your phone?" she asked obviously flustered. "It's the department."

"Sure, it's right over there," Carmen said pointing to the phone attached to the wall next to the refrigerator.

The phone rang almost on cue. Startled, they both jumped and looked at each other with alarm. Carmen picked up the receiver and glanced at her watch. She spoke briefly to the caller before setting it back onto the cradle.

"What's the matter?" Zoë demanded seeing the look of complete disbelief on Carmen's face.

"They just found another body and they're requesting our presence immediately," Carmen answered taking Zoë's hands into hers. "I told Chris to inform Captain Davis that you were with me and that we were on our way." Carmen paused for a moment trying to force her voice not to falter, "I can't believe he struck again so fast."

Zoë could not resist placing her arms around Carmen, "There is nothing we could have done to prevent this."

"I know," Carmen admitted.

"Are they sure it's the same guy?" Zoë questioned.

"I guess so," Carmen responded with a shrug. "Chris said that this victim was killed similar to the one downstairs and that there was another scribbled message left."

"So, how far away are we?" Zoë asked even though she knew it probably wasn't far.

"It's about twenty minutes from here."

"Well, Detective Moore, I guess we should put on our cop suits again," Zoë interjected trying to make the mood a little less tense.

"I'm sorry we have to leave in such a hurry," Carmen offered.

Zoë gave her best smile, "Why are you sorry? It isn't your fault."

"I know," Carmen acknowledged. "But, there's so much I need to say to you."

"And, there's so much I need to say to you," Zoë stressed fixing her blouse. "I do want to ask you something before we go though."

"Sure," Carmen agreed nervously. "What is it?"

"I'm not sure how you're feeling about what happened between us a few minutes ago," Zoë began wiping the palms of her hands on her jeans. "But, I would really like to take you out again. I mean, only if you want to go out again that is." With a nervous laugh, Zoë added; "God, I feel like a teenager trying to ask you to go steady."

Carmen wrapped her arms around Zoë. "I would love to go out again," she replied. "And, I'm not seeing anyone else, so I guess I could be your 'steady' if you wanted me too."

An expression of utter joy developed on Zoë's face and she couldn't resist kissing Carmen again. "I'd like that a lot," she cooed when their lips parted.

"Me, too," Carmen agreed. "Does this mean that there's a chance you'd like to have dinner with me tomorrow night?"

"I would love to," Zoë declared. "I can cook you dinner over at my condo and you can even brings Cuffs if you'd like."

"That sounds great. I can rent a movie if you have a DVD player."

"Sure," Zoë agreed moving toward the front door. "I can't remember the last time that I stayed home long enough to sit down. It would be nice spending an evening at home with you."

"Then, it's a date?" Carmen questioned hopefully.

"It's a date," Zoë confirmed.

With that, they left Carmen's apartment and headed toward the crime scene.

• • •

Carmen drove through the empty city streets. She turned onto the street that Chris had advised was the best route to take and checked in the rearview mirror to make sure Zoë was still behind her. Carmen knew she would have to block out her enjoyment of the previous few hours and get down to some serious detective work. "Lord, please let us find something to go on," she prayed touching the silver cross that dangled from her necklace. "We really need your help on this."

CHAPTER FOUR

The Mexican hacienda where the crime had occurred was located in an upscale housing development on the east side of town a few blocks from the beach on Rampart Road. A recently mowed, luscious green yard surrounded the residence. The hedges lining the front of the house were all trimmed back to below waist level. A lonely palm tree swayed from its position in the middle of the front yard with its full limbs rustling in the wind that was whipping over the rooftops. A red brick walkway led from the front entrance to the edge of the driveway where a pearly white BMW was parked.

At first glance, it might appear to a passerby that an officer's convention was taking place. The outer limits of the property were draped in yellow police tape. There were approximately seven marked squad cars, Duhn's unmarked car, the coroner's car, and the crime scene unit's van all parked strategically around the outer perimeter of the hacienda. A group of spectators had gathered in one of the adjoining properties where their jabbering could be heard over the thunder rumbling in the distance from an impending storm.

Carmen and Zoë parked across the street a few houses down from the crime scene. Carmen grabbed her flashlight and handheld radio from the trunk and waited for Zoë so that they could walk up together. She loved that it was a win-win situation for her because that's what she would have normally done with any detective assisting on a case. Still, she felt that everyone in a mile radius of her location knew that the two of them had kissed and what wicked thoughts she was harboring in the back of her mind.

Carmen noticed that as Zoë walked toward her one side of Zoë's shirt collar seemed to be slightly higher than the other one. She remembered Zoë's frantic attempt to button her shirt after their intimate encounter. Carmen smiled mischievously, "You might want to re-button your shirt. I think you missed one along the way."

"Well, Detective Moore," Zoë replied turning her back to Carmen. "While I'm good at chasing serial killers, I never claimed that I'm good at getting dressed quickly."

"Well, you never claimed that you're a good kisser," Carmen countered. "But, you are."

"And, so are you," Zoë grinned tucking her shirt back in.

They walked down the street toward the flashing red and blue lights. As they neared the curb, Chris emerged from the crime scene and strode across the lawn toward them. His hair was disheveled with one thick black strand sticking straight up in the middle of his head. He was wearing a white T-shirt with a Nike logo on it and a pair of crisp dark blue jeans.

"God, I am so glad you two are here!" he exclaimed transferring the worn scent of Preferred Stock cologne onto their clothing as he gave each of them a quick hug. "We need to put our heads together and find something to go on before this bastard strikes again. He's making us look like fools."

• • •

Zoë and Chris crossed through the yard and entered the hacienda through the front door. Carmen paused at the curb and studied the layout in front of her. She closed her eyes and cleared her thoughts. "If I were the killer," she thought. "What would be the first thing that I would do?"

She opened her eyes and headed over to the west side of the property. She stopped at the base of the driveway and switched on her flashlight. She swept the beam of light back and forth in front of her to look for any evidence that the killer might have dropped. As she approached the empty parking space next to the BMW, she noticed a dark spot about three feet away from the BMW's driver's side door. Squatting down, she peered at the black oily puddle that hadn't quite dried. She stepped over the spot and crouched beside the BMW. She peered underneath it and shined her flashlight on the undercarriage and then the ground.

She rose to her feet and removed the two-way radio clipped to her belt. "I need one of the crime scene technicians to come out to the driveway with a camera and collection kit," she ordered into the mike. "And, can anyone tell me if the victim had another vehicle?"

Instantly, the radio crackled, "On my way, Detective Moore," Debra informed. "I also have the information that you are inquiring about."

"10-4," Carmen replied. She positioned the flashlight in her right hand so that the beam illuminated the pages of the pocketsize notebook she had withdrawn from her jacket pocket. She skillfully drew a sketch of the front yard that included the shrubs, palm tree, and where the BMW was parked. She noted that there were no other oil marks anywhere else on the driveway. She placed her hand on the hood of the BMW and noted that it was not warm indicating the car had been sitting there for quite sometime.

"What do you have?" Debra called out to Carmen as she made her way down the red brick walkway.

"I need you take some pictures of the driveway and retrieve a sample of this substance," Carmen replied pointing down at the dark spot. "I want to verify what this is although I'm pretty sure it's oil."

"Sure, no problem" Debra said. "Leave it up to you to find something in almost complete darkness."

Carmen smiled and shrugged; "I guess when you're on the job as long as I've been, sometimes you just get lucky."

Debra rolled her eyes, "Carmen, you're one of the best detectives around, so don't feed me that line of bull."

"Whatever you say Debra, whatever you say," Carmen retorted with a smile.

Debra returned her smile before positioning herself at the optimal angle to take a snapshot of the substance on the driveway. She was an exceptional photographer and evidence technician and she took her work very seriously. She had been approached by various department heads insisting that she take the detective's exam, but she always refused. She had once confided in Carmen that if God had wanted her to risk her life, He wouldn't have blessed her with a husband and two wonderful kids. Carmen completely understood her position. It was the same one her own mother took when she had opted not to pursue a career in law enforcement.

"By the way, do we know if the victim owned another vehicle or not?" Carmen inquired, taking a minute to watch Debra work the evidence.

"No, she didn't," Debra replied without looking up. "At least, there are no other vehicles registered in her name."

Carmen headed for the front door again and continued to sweep her flashlight beam from left to right in a stubborn effort to find more evidence. She proceeded up to the brick walkway and examined it all the way to the front door. She turned to face the yard and noted that there was very little illumination. The front porch light was burnt out and the light escaping into the darkness from inside the house was just enough to throw eerie shadows on the walkway. The BMW was barely visible even though it was pearly white. She turned back around and examined the wooden doorframe. She noticed that there were no pry marks and the locks were still intact and seemed unscathed.

Carmen stepped into the living room and her foot was swallowed up by the deep blue cushioned carpeting. She glanced to her left and saw a light-blue couch angled slightly in front of a television set. There was a beautiful arrangement of pink carnations sitting in the middle of a rectangular coffee table and one wineglass half full sitting on a coaster. Carmen carefully made her way over to the coffee table and slipped on a latex glove that she had removed from her jacket pocket. She picked up the wine glass and examined the very distinctive lip outline left around the rim thanks to some exotic shade of red lipstick. She placed the glass back down onto the table and noticed a crossword puzzle magazine opened to page 23 that was unfinished.

She pivoted back around toward the doorway and was startled to see her own reflection in a mirror that hung flush against the wall just past the entryway. Feeling a little foolish, she took another look around the room before walking toward the sound of Mike's voice as it raised an octave higher to be heard over the crash of a lightening bolt that rattled the house.

Carmen had psyched herself up to make sure she was prepared for the scene that was laid out before her in the kitchen. The eviscerated body on top of the small round dining room table that seated two appeared to be an older

Hispanic woman. The victim still clenched the knife that the killer had placed in her left hand. Her eyelids had been taped open revealing bright red blood formations in the whites of her olive colored eyes, but there was too much blood to see if any bruising had formed around her neck. And, just like last time, the victim's hands had been wiped clean.

Carmen moved where Zoë, Chris, and Mike were conversing off to one side of the kitchen. She breathed through her mouth to avoid getting a whiff of death that filled the room. She pulled her Cross pen from the spiral wire wrapped around the top of the notebook. "Tell me what you have Mike," she demanded avoiding Zoë's watchful gaze.

"It appears to be the same guy, but I won't be a 100% sure until I do a thorough examination. That sick bastard even left another note," Mike exclaimed in disgust. "Chris had it photographed and placed into an evidence bag. We wrote down what it said because we knew that you would be interested in it."

"I'm definitely interested," Carmen assured without a moment's hesitation.

Chris looked down at his notes before inhaling a deep ragged breath. He cleared his throat and spoke the words as gently as possible:

"You'd better catch me and catch me fast.
I'm getting better at this detectives and it is
such a blast!"

The silence between the four of them spoke volumes in regard to what they were all feeling at the moment. Carmen's only reaction was the subtle tensing of her jaw muscle. She glanced at her wristwatch that told it was already 1:14 a.m. Time seemed to be moving full speed ahead and they still weren't any closer to catching the guy. Finally, she broke the eerie quiet that had settled over them and the tiredness in her voice was evident, "Chris, did you find anything else that might help us?"

"Not really," he remarked, fighting off a yawn. "But, then again, I haven't had a chance to interview any of the neighbors yet. I assigned Sgt. Hammond to do some initial questioning and I thought we could do the follow-ups."

"Well, let's get to it," Carmen suggested. "It doesn't seem like our perpetrator is taking a rest between kills, so neither will we."

"We have a serial killer on our hands, don't we?" Chris interjected already knowing the answer.

"Yep," Zoë confirmed. "And, we better start making some serious strides in the investigation."

"We will," Carmen assured. "Are you going to assist Mike in examining the victim?"

"Of course," Zoë replied slapping Mike on the back. "We're going to conquer that mountain together."

"Though I don't share Zoë's enthusiasm," Mike remarked. "I'll call you right after I finish the examination."

"That works for me."

Carmen glanced over at the victim. Truth be known, she desperately wanted to have a closer look at the body, but she didn't want anyone to feel that she doubted their investigative abilities. She knew that solving a case was all about trusting the people you worked with. Besides, she would receive an excellent autopsy report from Mike as soon as he was finished. "Thanks," she offered before walking out of the room with Chris beside her.

Carmen stopped briefly at the mirror that she had noticed earlier and scoffed at her appearance. She, too, had dark circles under her eyes. She ran her fingers through her hair to try and give it a little bit of lift, but it fell back down. She shook her head and turned toward the door. But, out of the corner of her eye, she caught a glimpse of something near the bottom of the mirror that caused her heart to skip a beat. Taking a closer look, she realized that there was a large smudge on the lower right hand corner of the mirror. "Look at this, Chris!" she exclaimed. "I think it's a fingerprint."

Bewildered, Chris leaned over her shoulder and cocked his head to one side, "How in the world did you see that?"

"Well, I didn't notice it at first," she stated, her excitement unable to be harnessed. "In fact, I didn't even see the mirror until I turned around from inspecting the coffee table over there when I first got here."

"It's a large smudge," Chris stated. "Do you really think our killer would be so careless?"

"The mirror is almost flush with the wall. I'm surprised I didn't bump into it when I first came in," Carmen revealed. "I just now decided to see how awful I looked before starting these interviews."

"Okay," Chris said skeptically. "What's your theory?"

"Suppose the killer conned his way in and went to close the door behind him," she speculated.

"Haven't we proven that the killer wears gloves?" he questioned.

"It's August, Chris," she replied, her eyes sparkling. "Who wears gloves in Florida in August?"

"You have a point."

"And, do you feel the temperature in here?"

"It's cool," he answered. "So?"

"The air conditioning is on," she stated. "Maybe the victim asked him to close the door."

"And, he wasn't expecting that," Chris interjected thoughtfully. "He probably didn't see the mirror when he reached back to close the door."

"And, he closed it without his gloves on," Carmen concluded triumphantly.

"Leave it up to a woman to find a fingerprint when she's trying to primp," Chris mused giving her a light jab with his elbow in the ribcage.

"I think you meant to say leave it up to the brilliance of a woman to find evidence even while primping," Carmen corrected.

"Hey Debra," Chris said into his radio as he winked at Carmen, "I need you back inside when you're finished with the driveway. We found something of interest."

When Debra arrived, Chris pointed out the fingerprint and she photographed it right away. Carmen walked back over to the coffee table and carefully picked up the crossword puzzle book. She glanced at the previous pages and saw that the crosswords had all been completed. At the top of each page there was a date written. On the page just before the one left open, the victim had written the previous day's date. The rest of the pages, Carmen realized, also had the dates noted in consecutive order since the beginning of the month. On page 23, today's date would have been written, but the victim never had the chance to finish the crossword.

Carmen felt the anger swell inside of her for the man who had done this and she bolted out the front door. She was halfway across the street when Chris finally caught up with her. "Hey, you all right?" he asked worriedly.

"It just pisses me off! Two nights! It has only been two nights!" she hissed. "What the hell is this guy's motive?"

"I don't know," he admitted. "But even though the situation seems a little bleak, we'll find a connection. We always do, don't we?"

Deep down, Carmen knew Chris was right. Keeping a positive attitude was an essential part of the investigation.

Carmen walked over to Sgt. Hammond, who was waiting for her next to his patrol car. "So did you find anything out from the neighbors?" she asked, half expecting the answer to be a quick 'no'.

"Well, the Delaney's who live next door to the victim advised that they didn't hear or see anything," Sgt. Hammond stated. "But, the Knights who live right across the street said that their seventeen-year old daughter might have some information that could be helpful."

"I sure hope so," Carmen replied. "Keep up the good work."

"I will," Sgt. Hammond replied, puffing out his chest slightly.

Carmen and Chris made their way to the only house with its front porch light still on. They climbed the steps leading up to the Knight's front door as the wind was starting to kick up again. The temperature was falling and lightening flashed through the night sky in horizontal bursts. As Carmen raised her hand to knock on the door, it swung open and a brown-eyed boy around the age of ten screamed, "Mom! They're here!"

"Well, let them in," an older woman's voice bellowed from somewhere inside the residence. "I'll be there in a minute."

The little boy stepped aside and allowed Carmen and Chris to enter. As they waited by the entryway, the little boy bombarded them with questions. "Are you guys really cops? Do you know who did it yet? Did you dust for fingerprints and everything like they do on TV?"

Before Carmen or Chris could even respond, a petite woman with dishwater blond hair entered the room. She was in her early forties and slightly overweight just in the hip area indicating she probably had a desk job. "You leave those two alone and get ready for bed," Mrs. Knight instructed. "It is way past your bed time."

"Ah mom, I didn't even get to find out if there was blood or anything," the little boy whined showing the innocence of his age.

"Get upstairs young man or I will have your hide for even thinking of such a question!"

The young boy raced up the stairs. A few seconds later, a door slammed from somewhere on the second floor. Mrs. Knight turned her attention back to Carmen and Chris and her blue eyes traveled back and forth between them. Carmen could tell that behind the brave front this woman was determined to show, she was terrified for her family.

Mrs. Knight tapped her right pointer finger against her chin for a moment. "I don't mind you talking to Natalie," she stated. "But, don't try to intimidate her. She mowed that woman's lawn whenever it needed it and I know they had a good rapport. She is really upset and it took me a long time to calm her down."

Carmen sympathized with the mother's standpoint. "Mrs. Knight," she began compassionately, "we just want to ask your daughter what she might have seen and approximately at what time. That's all."

"Okay, but I'll be in the next room," Mrs. Knight reiterated. "I'll give you as much privacy as you need, but if she decides not to talk to you, I will completely back that decision. Understand?"

"Completely," Chris agreed.

Mrs. Knight turned abruptly and left the room. Chris sat down in an old rocker that creaked under his weight. Blushing slightly, he whispered, "Do you think it will hold me?"

Carmen grinned fiendishly, "We will see, won't we?"

Carmen settled herself into a brightly flowered loveseat. A young girl with brown curly hair entered the room with three glasses and a pitcher of lemonade. Her eyes were swollen and she still had red blotches on her face from crying. She carefully sat the tray down beside Carmen. "I know it's not coffee, but I thought you all might like something to drink," Natalie offered pouring a glass of lemonade. "Is that okay?"

"It's perfect," Carmen assured taking the glass of lemonade from the girl's shaking hands.

"We just appreciate that you are so willing to talk to us," Chris chimed in, keeping his tone friendly.

"Ms. Lopez was my friend," Natalie blurted out angrily. "I can't believe something had to happen to someone so nice."

"That's why we're trying to find out who did this, so we can stop them before he or she hurts another nice person," Carmen stressed.

"And, that's the reason we need you," Chris added. "We were told that you might have seen something that might help us."

"I really don't know if any of what I saw will be important," Natalie concluded, her voice trailing off.

Carmen wasn't sure if Natalie would be able to go on. "Just take your time," Carmen instructed gently. "We're in no rush."

Natalie took a deep quivering breath, "I got home about 9:00 p.m. from basketball practice. I noticed that Ms. Lopez had a van parked in her driveway. I thought that was sort of unusual because she wasn't too fond of people dropping by late at night," she stated solemnly. "Curiosity finally got the better of me and I called over there. When I didn't get an answer, I just figured maybe she finally met a nice guy and wanted a quiet evening at home without interruption, you know?"

"I know," Carmen agreed.

Tears sprang to Natalie's eyes and she placed her hands over her face. "Do you think if I would have went over there I could have saved her?" she sobbed.

Carmen squeezed the girl's hand. "You would have probably been hurt too," she said softly. "Besides, you're helping her right now because without you we wouldn't have any leads at all."

Natalie looked up at Carmen with huge sorrowful brown eyes and wiped her nose with a tissue. "I guess it was about 9:20 when I looked out my window again and saw that the van was gone," she recalled. "I tried to call Ms. Lopez again, but no one answered. I thought maybe she had left with him."

"Did you notice what color the van was or anything else unusual?" Chris inquired gently.

"I think it was brown, but I'm not positive," she stated. "This street isn't lit real well at night if you've noticed."

"We've noticed," Carmen interjected.

Natalie grew silent for a moment, obviously lost in deep thought. "Ms. Lopez was pretty predictable," she whispered. "Every night she would do her crossword puzzles, pull her car in, and then go to bed. She did that same routine every night."

"That's extremely useful information," Chris praised.

Natalie struggled to keep herself from crying again causing her voice to crackle as she continued. "She was pretty safety minded too. She always locked her front door and would only unlock it if she knew the person or was getting a delivery."

"A delivery? Like what kind?" Carmen inquired glancing over at Chris.

"The usual stuff," Natalie said with a shrug. "She would order stuff from one of the shopping channels or get her groceries delivered. Things like that."

"Does she have any family members living close by that you know of?" Carmen prodded, still maintaining her genial tone.

"Her sister lives just on the outskirts of town," Natalie replied. "I gave Sgt. Hammond, I think that's his name, the information. He said he was going to send an officer over there to tell her what happened. I can give you the information if you want me to."

"That won't be necessary. I'll get it from the Sergeant in just a little while. Besides, it's late and we need to let you get to bed," Carmen professed, genuinely concerned for Natalie's well being.

"Yeah, I have school tomorrow," Natalie said proudly. "I'm about to finish my junior year and I've managed to maintain a 4.0 average."

"That's terrific," Chris exclaimed. "Keep up the good work."

"I will," she said confidently.

"Alright," Carmen interrupted reaching into her pocket and pulling out a silver business card holder. "If you remember anything else or you think you see that van again, you can call me day or night, okay?" Carmen removed one of her business cards and scribbled her cell phone number on the back of it before handing it to Natalie.

"Sure, Detective Moore, no problem," Natalie replied.

"You can call me Carmen, okay?"

"Sure, Carmen," Natalie said softly.

"Do you have any questions for us?" Chris interjected almost in a fatherly tone as he got his feet.

"Do you think you could have an officer drive by our house a little more often?" Natalie inquired nervously. "It would sure make me feel a whole lot safer."

"For you, I think we can arrange that," Carmen stated giving Natalie a hug. "I promise that we will catch him."

"I know you will," Natalie replied.

With that, Carmen and Chris saw themselves out. They walked into the brisk night air with heavy hearts and troubled minds. Carmen turned around and waived at Natalie who was staring out the living room window. She returned the wave and vanished back behind the curtain. Tiny droplets of rain began falling as if the heavens were crying from the loss of another innocent to the cruel realities that the world spawned.

CHAPTER FIVE

Carmen pulled her keys out of her pocket, waved goodbye to Chris, and jumped inside her car. She turned the key in the ignition and listened as her engine hummed quietly. The clock on the radio display showed 3:05 a.m. Raindrops splattered heavily against the windshield and another bolt of lightning lit up the night sky. She rested her chin on the steering wheel and watched as Ms. Lopez's body, sealed in a waterproof bag, was wheeled out of her home.

Zoë had left about ten minutes earlier at the insistence of her captain to get some rest before the following day. He wanted her to be refreshed and ready to tackle the mountain of evidence that had been collected by the crime scene unit. Debra and her team had volunteered to work through the night analyzing and processing their findings. They were dedicated to their jobs. But, it was the memory of the victims that drove them to work harder and strive for perfection.

Carmen knew that Debra would have the film from the crime scene developed and ready for her to pick up before dawn. The latent print examiner, Daniel Wright, would more than likely have the fingerprint that was lifted from the mirror analyzed and ran through AFIS before the morning as well. He almost always found a match. If this method wasn't successful though, it was up to the detectives to find the person to whom the fingerprint belonged. The rest of the crime scene technicians would be busy comparing blood samples, hair samples, and partaking in various other tasks.

Carmen started the engine and pulled away from the curb. She drove slowly past the Knight's home. She wondered if Natalie had been able to fall asleep. She knew that Natalie would probably never again feel safe in that neighborhood or in her house for that matter. Who could blame her? Carmen didn't feel entirely safe in her own apartment complex and she was a cop. Whoever was responsible for these vicious crimes, knew exactly when and where to strike and was skilled enough to leave no evidence behind.

Carmen's thoughts inevitably turned to Zoë. She could still smell her sweet perfume lingering on her skin. The tenderness she had experienced while in Zoë's arms earlier in the evening was mesmerizing. Still, she couldn't help but wonder why Zoë hadn't waited on her or at the very least said goodbye. Carmen picked up her cell phone and checked to see if she had received any messages. Disappointed, she dialed dispatch and the smooth sexy masculine voice that answered the line recognized her voice immediately.

"Detective Moore, what can I do for you?" Tim, the lead dispatcher, prodded.

"Well, let me fantasize about that for a while," she teased. "Right now, I was wondering if you could tell me if Detective Childers has called off duty."

"Yes, about 10 minutes ago."

"Thanks Tim," she replied. "And, I'm still fantasizing."

He chuckled softly, "It's not nice to give false hope to old friends."

"It hasn't been that long since we were in high school together," Carmen countered.

"Yeah, what's thirteen years?" Tim snickered.

"We are old, aren't we?" Carmen responded. "I'll be forty in eight years!"

"I'll be forty in seven years," Tim retorted. "So, stop it already."

"Alright," Carmen replied. "I'll see you later."

Carmen closed her cell phone and made a right hand turn onto Oceanview Parkway. She pulled up to the curb across the street from her apartment complex and switched off the engine. She peered up at her bedroom window and knew without a doubt that she was going to have to move when her lease came due. She could deal with the violence and death at work; she was a homicide detective after all. But, she didn't want to have to deal with it at home too. And, to make matters worse, she felt as though she had let the residents down somehow and that was eating her alive inside.

She reached behind the passenger seat and searched for the handle of her briefcase. Her fingertips brushed against the cool metal clasps on top of the case and she casually glanced out the back window. She froze instantly. A dark colored van was parked along the side of the street in the shadows about two blocks away. Somewhat alarmed, she tried to resist her paranoia, but the coincidence was just too creepy.

She opened the glove compartment and removed a pair of binoculars from within. She raised them to her eyes and focused in on the van's front windshield. She could see that someone was in the driver's seat smoking a cigarette. She tried to adjust her position, but as fate would have it, her head brushed against the dome light and switched it on. The van's headlights instantly turned on blinding her. She dropped the binoculars into her lap and instinctively placed her hands in front of her eyes.

Carmen couldn't see the imminent danger that she was in. The van barreled toward her and the driver leaned out the side window taking aim with a 9mm Beretta. Within seconds, he would have a perfect head shot and Carmen wouldn't even have time to know what hit her. But, Carmen's gut instinct told her that she was a sitting duck. So, she crawled into the passenger seat still unable to see and reached for the door handle.

A sudden crash of metal against metal filled the air. It was followed by another crash and the explosive exchange of gunfire. Bullets slammed into the Corvette and Carmen could hear them ricocheting within its shell. She opened the car door and fell onto the ground. She removed the Glock 40 from the holster still tucked into her jeans and squatted beside the tire well to listen.

She stayed hidden as the sounds of shattering glass and metal grinding into the pavement were followed by the roar of an engine and the squealing of tires. The final act of whatever chaotic event that had just occurred subsided. Carmen carefully eased her head up above the hood of the car and glanced quickly from side to side before ducking back down again. She still had bright white dots from the van's headlights interfering with her vision.

Carmen peeked up again and looked down the road. There, lying on its side about 30 yards away, was a dark blue Blazer. As the white voids in her vision faded, Carmen read the license tag that was illuminated just enough by a brightly lit street light. Her heart felt as though one of the bullets had struck her in the chest shredding it into a million pieces. The plate spelled out 'Childrs' in black lettering. "Zoë!" she gasped springing to her feet.

Carmen didn't realize she was running until she was almost at the Blazer's bumper. Nor, did she notice the police cruiser screeching to a halt 15 feet behind her. All she cared about was getting to Zoë. The rest of the world would just have to wait.

Officer Tom Leigh jumped out of his cruiser with radio in hand. "I need medical assistance at the corner of Oceanview Parkway and Granite Avenue," he shouted. "We have an officer down."

Leigh, who was of Irish decent, had fair skin and green eyes adding to his already boyish look. He had an impressive physique documented by the various weightlifting competitions he had won in his weight class. He had amazing speed for his 5'5" frame and he caught up to Carmen in record time without breaking a sweat. He grabbed Carmen by the arm and pulled her away as she tried to maneuver through the jagged pieces of glass that surrounded what was left of the back windshield of the Blazer.

"What the hell are you doing?" Carmen shrieked. "Get your fucking hands off of me! I have to get to her!"

"Detective Moore, listen to me," Leigh commanded respectfully. "We need to find out where she is in the vehicle. If we go in there blind, we'll get hurt and that won't help her."

Carmen stepped back realizing he was right. She needed to slow down and not panic. She noticed that her Glock was still in her hand and she immediately secured it in the holster. Leigh began hollering into the damp night air, "Zoë, can you hear me?" He pulled his flashlight off his belt and hurried to the front of the Blazer. "Answer me or I'll kick your ass!" he shouted.

A slight rustling could be heard from within the Blazer and then a low moan. Carmen and Leigh held their breaths. "You and what army is going to kick my ass?" Zoë inquired in a labored tone.

Carmen and Leigh breathed a sigh of relief and attempted to see Zoë through the busted up windshield. But, the Blazer had started filling with smoke and along with dissipating visibility they were also losing precious time. Leigh climbed up on top of the Blazer's side and pried open the driver's side door that was heavily damaged. He shined his flashlight down into the interior and could see Zoë lying against the passenger side door covered in glass. The upper right side of Zoë's shirt was soaked in blood.

"Is Carmen alright?" Zoë grunted through a clenched jaw.

"Yeah, she's alright," Leigh acknowledged. "What's important now is getting you out of there as soon as possible."

"How is she?" Carmen prodded, feeling totally helpless as she waited impatiently on the ground.

Leigh looked down at Carmen as he balanced precariously on the Blazer, "She's bleeding pretty badly."

"We have to get her out of there," Carmen replied.

Smoke was now billowing out of the open door causing Leigh's eyes and nose to water. Zoë was coughing uncontrollably. Leigh hooked his flashlight back onto his belt and straddled the frame of the door. "Give me your hand," he commanded reaching down to Zoë.

Zoë peered up at him dejectedly, but he smiled reassuringly, "I know you can do this." Suddenly, the Blazer's engine erupted into a fireball. "Holy shit!" Leigh yelled overcome by fear. "Come on Zoë, grab my hand!"

Carmen sprinted over to Leigh's cruiser and yanked open the door. She pulled the release lever for the trunk and grabbed the fire extinguisher out of it. She raced back over to the Blazer and pulled the pin on the fire extinguisher. She aimed and squeezed the handle dousing the engine with carbon dioxide, but it seemed to help as much as if she had spit on it.

Leigh pulled Zoë out of the opening just as the flames found their way through the dashboard. Carmen tossed the empty fire extinguisher aside and helped Leigh lower Zoë onto the ground. Carmen placed Zoë's right arm around her shoulder and wrapped her left arm around Zoë's waist. Leigh scrambled down off the Blazer and placed his arm behind Zoë's back grabbing a hold of one of the belt loops on her jeans. Together, Carmen and Leigh hoisted Zoë up and quickly carried her away from the impending explosion.

• • •

Three more cruisers and another fire truck responded to the scene. Within a half an hour, the charred remains of Zoë's Blazer were 'resting in peace' on top of a tow truck. Carmen hadn't been able to speak to Zoë or see how she was doing since her boss, Captain Davis, had arrived on the scene. He had taken immediate control and ordered Carmen away from Zoë's side with the instructions to give a statement to one of the officers in charge of reconstructing the accident. Since then, he had been quietly talking with Zoë and taking notes.

Carmen needed to hold Zoë in her arms and tell her everything was going to be okay. Why did Captain Davis have to be such a jerk? Restlessly, Carmen continued to watch the paramedics work on Zoë from a distance. When she noticed Leigh putting the empty fire extinguisher back into his trunk, she strutted up behind him and tapped him on the shoulder. "I'm so sorry for…"

"There's no need for an apology," Leigh interrupted turning around and placing his index finger gently on her lips to quiet her. "I have no clue what happened tonight, but I know that there are two bullet holes in the driver's side door of your car. All I want to know is what the hell happened? If you can tell me that, than that's all that matters."

"The thing is," Carmen revealed regretfully, "I don't have any idea what happened. In a nutshell, I noticed a van a couple blocks away and was temporarily blinded by his headlights. Then, I heard metal grinding together and gunfire. I wish I knew more to tell you."

"Well," Leigh replied turning back around and closing the trunk lid. "I've had all the excitement I want for one night. I'm going home to my wonderful wife who I'm sure has been listening to all of this chaos on the scanner."

"I'm sure," Carmen agreed.

"She's text messaged me about four times saying she loves me since this thing started," he stated with a smile. "So, I'd be willing to bet money that she's been listening."

"I'd take that bet if I wasn't sure to lose," Carmen said. "Scanners are such a double-edged sword for families anyway."

"You've got that right," Leigh replied. "They get the thrill of hearing you answer calls and arrest the bad guys. But, they also have the equal chance of hearing you get hurt or something worse."

"True," Carmen agreed sullenly.

"On that happy note," Leigh said sarcastically. "I'm going home. Let me know if you find out anything and how Zoë is doing?"

"Of course," Carmen reassured. "Thanks again for all your help."

"Well, besides it being my job to back up my fellow officers," he stated. "I happen to think you're pretty okay."

"I think you're pretty okay, too," Carmen complimented shaking Leigh's hand.

Leigh stepped up to the driver's side door. He paused as if debating on what to do next. Then, he looked over at

Carmen and smiled. "By the way," he confided, "the first thing Zoë asked me was if you were alright. I just thought you might want to know that."

"Thanks," Carmen replied, "I owe you one."

"Nah, just watch your back, okay?"

"Sure," Carmen said. "Now, go home and get some rest."

Leigh got into his patrol car and drove off. Carmen watched him until the taillights of his cruiser disappeared around a corner about three blocks away. She turned around in time to see the ambulance that Zoë was in leave the scene and head toward the hospital. She made a beeline toward the apartment complex to make sure Cuffs was okay and to call Chris. When she reached the sidewalk in front of her building, Captain Davis hurried up to her and pulled her aside.

"I need to speak with you for a minute," he ordered.

"You can speak with me," Carmen said coolly, "but I suggest removing your hand from around my arm."

"Zoë told me that this all started when she decided to investigate a dark colored van sitting just down the street from your apartment," Captain Davis stated releasing his grip. "According to the officer you talked to, you didn't see a whole hell of a lot. Did you see the van or did you miss that too?"

Carmen was infuriated. Every muscle in her body was itching to slap this man across the face, but she refrained. Squaring her shoulders, she looked him straight in the eyes, "I saw the van, but like I told the officer, I wasn't planning on getting shot at tonight. I didn't even know Zoë was anywhere around."

Captain Davis studied Carmen's facial expression for a moment and his tone lightened, "I'm sorry Detective

Moore. I know I am way out of line, but you have to understand that I feel more like Zoë's father than her boss."

Surprised, Carmen didn't dare interrupt. "She's my best friend's daughter," Captain Davis said softly. "I've basically watched her grow up. So if I was hard on you, I'm sorry. I just want to nail the person responsible for this."

"It's alright," Carmen replied, never imagining Captain Davis was being rude to her out of concern for Zoë. "I'm sorry too," she offered feeling like a self-righteous feminist. "I thought you didn't want me around for a different reason."

Captain Davis' eyebrows raised and an ornery grin touched his lips. He looked around suspiciously and waved his finger at Carmen to come closer. "I've known Zoë was a lesbian since she was seventeen," he admitted frankly. "She tells me everything. And yesterday, she called to tell me that she was taking you out."

"She did?" Carmen asked bewildered.

Amused by the utter disbelief on Carmen's face, he offered her an ultimatum. "So, do you want to discuss that or would you like to hear what she told me about what happened tonight?"

"What, uh, happened tonight?" Carmen squeaked.

"Apparently, she was going to stop by to see you when she saw the van. She thought it was a little suspicious so she continued past your apartment and did a little backtracking. She turned up an alleyway that intersected directly behind where the van was parked. She killed her lights and eased up behind it. She hit Officer Leigh on the tactical channel to back her up. Then, she saw you pass by."

Inhaling a long deep breath, Captain Davis peered up at the clear night sky. He clasped his hands together and arched his arms above his head to stretch. "At first, Zoë thought the driver saw her. But, as she gave chase, the suspect aimed what she believed was a pistol out his window toward your car. She gunned her vehicle and nailed his back bumper, but he was able to get a couple shots off."

Captain Davis wiped the beads of sweat off his forehead. "She also stated that she swerved to the right of the van and managed to get beside it," he continued. "The van slammed into the side of her Blazer and the suspect fired a few shots at her. She returned fire, but none of the bullets hit their mark. The suspect kept ramming the side of her Blazer until it finally flipped onto its' side. After that, Zoë just remembers hearing Leigh's voice calling her name."

"Well, I think the person we're looking for in connection with these murders was the one driving the van," Carmen stated.

"You're probably right, so I wouldn't stay here tonight if I were you," Captain Davis warned. "That guy has a lot of balls going after a cop. And the pressure will be on since he may think you saw him."

"I'm going to the hospital to check on Zoë anyway," Carmen replied. "I'll make arrangements to stay at a friend's house before I go."

"That sounds like a wise decision," he said. "Please tell Zoë to call me if she needs anything."

"I will," Carmen promised.

"By the way, we need to process your car," Captain Davis informed. "So, will you give your car key to one of the officers?"

"Sure," she replied. "There's nothing like getting shot at to insure a new paint job."

"That's true," Captain Davis remarked. "But, didn't you just get this car?"

"Last year."

"Well, it's beautiful," he said admiringly. "They'll probably only have to replace the door."

"I hope so," Carmen replied trying to keep her tone from reflecting her building impatience. "Are we finished here?"

"Yes," he answered, "if you promise me that you'll be careful."

"Don't worry about me, Captain," Carmen said shaking his hand. "I have it all under control."

She walked over to her Corvette and motioned one of the remaining officers left at the scene to join her. The young new recruit jogged over to her in his crisp blue uniform. He almost stood at attention in front of her. "Yes Detective Moore, did you need something?" he inquired.

Carmen loved new recruits for two reasons. One, they were usually very polite, and two, they were always willing to help. "My car is part of the crime scene," she stated opening the driver's side door. "Can you see to it that it gets processed and that I'm notified the moment I can get it back?"

"No problem," he stated. "Anything else?"

"I'm going to go up to my apartment and get a few things," she replied removing the car key from her key ring and handing it to him. "Contact Detective Duhn and tell him to pick me up in about 15 minutes. Also, let him know that I need him to keep my dog for the rest of the night."

"Yes, ma'am," the new recruit replied spinning on his heels and dutifully heading back to his cruiser.

Carmen reached behind the driver's seat and picked up her briefcase. She closed the door and ran her fingers against the two bullet holes that were embedded just below and to the left of the door handle. She shook her head trying to ward of the nauseous feeling at the realization that she could have been killed. She hurried across the street and up the steps to the entrance of her apartment complex. Not wanting to waste any time, she ran up all seven flights of stairs. Her every thought consisted of Zoë. She put her key into the deadbolt and unlocked the door. "Please let her be all right," she whispered.

Cuffs jumped at Carmen's legs as soon as she walked in. She set her briefcase down beside the door and scooped him up into her arms. She scratched the inside of his right ear and made her way to the bedroom. She set Cuffs on the bed and walked over to the closet. She pulled out her duffel bag and began tossing clothes into it not having any idea how much or how little to pack.

About 10 minutes later, she was ready to go. She picked up Cuffs with her left hand and tossed the navy blue duffel bag over her right shoulder. She turned off every light except for the one in the kitchen. She grabbed her briefcase, closed the front door, and locked it. She predicted that Chris would already be waiting for her downstairs. She pushed the 'down' button and within seconds the elevator doors opened.

As she and Cuffs descended, the thought occurred to her that if Zoë hadn't been there, she would definitely be the one in hospital or worse, the morgue. "Thank you, God," she whispered. "I've always needed an 'angel in blue' so to speak to save me."

Chris was waiting inside the front entrance when Carmen stepped off the elevator. He quickly grabbed the duffel bag off her shoulder and the briefcase from her hand. "Honey, are you alright?" he asked, hugging her.

"I'm fine," she assured. "Can you drop me off at the hospital and look after Cuffs for me for a little while?"

"Sure," Chris agreed without hesitation. "What the heck happened tonight?"

"I don't have the answers and I'm too tired to speculate," she pleaded as exhaustion raged war on her body. "So, could we possibly discuss this tomorrow?"

Chris nodded his head in agreement and placed his arm around her waist. He led her out to his car and opened the passenger side door. Carmen buckled herself in and Cuffs made himself comfortable on her lap. Chris hurried over to the other side and tossed the duffle bag and briefcase behind the driver's seat. He climbed in, started the engine, and tuned the radio to a country music station, which he knew was Carmen's favorite. He maneuvered the sedan away from the curb and headed toward the hospital.

Chris kept a close watch on Carmen as she drifted off to sleep. When they arrived at the hospital, he gently shook her. "Carmen, we're here," he announced softly.

"Thanks buddy," she answered wearily, leaning over and kissing him on the cheek.

"Are you going to be alright?" he asked, accepting Cuffs into his arms.

"I'll be fine," she replied, reaching into the backseat to retrieve the duffle bag and briefcase.

"Cuffs can stay with us as long as you need him to," Chris offered. "And, Mary said that you're more than welcome to stay in our guest room."

"You're the best," Carmen replied. "And, I'll let you know what I plan on doing when I figure that out."

"Okay, but if you need anything, don't hesitate to call."

"I won't," she replied, opening the passenger side door.

Cuffs tilted his head to one side as if wondering where she was going without him. Carmen leaned over and patted him on the head. "You be a good boy for Uncle Chris," she whispered. "I'll come get you real soon." With that, she closed the passenger side door and hurried through the sliding glass doors that led into the emergency room.

• • •

Zoë was instantly aware of the intense pain in her right shoulder as she forced herself to wake. Her eyelids felt extremely swollen. She struggled to lift them and the light that escaped through the narrow slits caused her head to hurt. She could sense someone holding her hand and she forced her eyes open the rest of the way to see who it might be. She felt her heart smile, but before she could say one word to Carmen, she was in dreamland again.

Carmen continued to hold Zoë's hand throughout the early morning hours. She had used her badge to secure her place beside Zoë's side since visiting hours didn't begin until 8 a.m. She had contacted the admitting emergency room nurse and learned that Zoë had received 32 stitches in her right shoulder and sustained a mild concussion. She kept close tabs on the equipment monitoring Zoë's vital signs and refused to give in to the exhaustion that seemed to be crashing down on her in waves.

About 7:30 a.m., the nightshift nurse left a breakfast tray beside the bed for Zoë in case she woke up. She also brought Carmen another cup of coffee. Carmen graciously accepted and downed it in less than five minutes. Eventually, Carmen laid her head down on the edge of the bed about 8:00 a.m. and drifted off. About 10 minutes before noon, she felt someone playing with her hair. Her eyes drifted up to Zoë's face.

Zoë, still under the influence of pain medication, offered a faint smile. Overjoyed, Carmen instantly leaned forward to kiss her. Their lips were mere inches of each other when a pretty nurse with long jet black hair pulled back in a ponytail strolled through the door with lunch. Startled, Carmen almost fell out of the chair feeling like a deer caught in headlights.

The nurse giggled and placed the lunch tray onto the adjustable cart. "Good morning sunshine," she greeted.

"Good morning," Zoë replied picking up her fork and stabbing the slices of turkey with it. "So, are you going to tell me how I look, Linda?"

"Well, you've looked better," the nurse replied sarcastically. "But, I guess you're presentable."

"I know I can always count on you to give me an honest opinion," Zoë stated, struggling to sit up a little bit straighter.

"So, what happened this time?" Linda pressed. "I heard through the grapevine that you were trying to protect some damsel in distress again. I hope she was worth the trouble."

"She was," Zoë said simply, winking at Carmen.

"Are you going to introduce me to your new friend?" Linda asked acknowledging Carmen's presence.

"This is the damsel in distress," Zoë introduced, "although she prefers to go by Detective Moore. Carmen, this is my sister, Linda."

Blushing, Linda stuck out her hand, "I'm so sorry if I offended you. I just worry about her."

"I completely understand," Carmen stated easily shaking Linda's hand. "Besides, in a way, I was that damsel in distress. If your sister hadn't been there, I would probably be wearing a toe tag right now."

"Don't say things like that," Zoë declared protectively.

"It's the truth," Carmen countered.

"Well, the doctor said you can check out whenever you're feeling up to it," Linda interjected. "But, you are to stay off work for a few days and get plenty of rest. I'll come over and help change the bandages on your shoulder unless someone else is going to be there with you."

"I'll be just fine," Zoë replied. "Carmen can take care of changing the bandages and I can call if I need you to come over, okay?"

"Alright," Linda agreed. "You just make sure you keep an eye out for infection. That cut was pretty deep."

"Will do sis! I'll be good, I promise," Zoë mocked in a childish voice.

"It was very nice to meet you, Carmen," Linda stated, rolling her eyes in response to Zoë's behavior. "Take care of my sister and don't let her give you any crap. I'll call later to see how she's doing."

With that, Linda was out the door pushing the food cart down the hallway once again. Carmen avoided Zoë's eyes and reached for the soup container on the lunch tray. "We should probably remove the lid, so that it will cool down," she whispered.

Zoë gently grabbed Carmen's wrist and pulled her closer. "I was so afraid you had gotten hurt," Zoë began. "It just happened so fast and I didn't have time to do anything, but..." Zoë was stopped mid-sentence as Carmen kissed her.

Carmen slowly pulled away and nuzzled her head down onto Zoë's chest. "If it weren't for you, I would probably have two bullet holes in my head. You had perfect timing."

"I wouldn't say perfect timing," Zoë countered. "He still got some shots off."

Carmen looked up at Zoë quizzically, "By the way, why were you there?"

Surprised by the question, Zoë stumbled for words. "Well, I...You see, I thought I would make sure you got home okay. That's all."

"So, you were worried about me, huh?" Carmen asked attempting to sound as nonchalant about it as possible.

"I was just concerned," Zoë explained, avoiding Carmen's eyes. "I happen to care, you know?"

"I know," Carmen replied. "I happen to care about you, too."

CHAPTER SIX

It had taken almost forty-five minutes in the mid-afternoon traffic to reach Zoë's three-bedroom condo on the North side of town. Carmen handed the taxi driver two twenty dollar bills and helped Zoë out of the back of the cab. Zoë stumbled up the three steps onto the porch and unlocked the front door. She punched in the five digit code that disengaged the burglar alarm and motioned Carmen to follow her. She staggered across the living room floor and disappeared into an adjoining room.

Carmen closed the front door and secured the deadbolt. She looked around the room and marveled at the sophistication of the furnishings and the immaculate hardwood flooring. Along the walls, there were hand-painted pictures of dolphins and the ocean. A four tier china cabinet with exquisitely sculpted glass figurines of all sorts of sea-dwelling creatures was nestled in the far left corner. In the middle of the room, a stylish Persian rug lay in front of a fireplace with a blush-beige sectional couch surrounding it.

Carmen walked over to the adjoining room and peeked around the corner. Zoë was sprawled out on a king-size platform bed sound asleep. A beautiful oriental red bedspread was folded neatly back revealing the crumpled up white satiny sheets that shimmered from the sunshine seeping through the window blinds. Carmen tiptoed over to the bed and brushed back the hair that had fallen in front of Zoë's eyes. She grabbed the top sheet feeling the silkiness between her fingers and pulled it up around Zoë's shoulders. Then she got to her feet, adjusted the blinds to darken the room, and quietly closed the bedroom door behind her.

Carmen crossed back through the living room and passed by the kitchen. She had some investigating to do and the kitchen was at the bottom of the list. She came to the first door to the left of the kitchen and opened it. It was a full-size bathroom decorated in brilliant shades of brown, gold, and green. There was a huge garden tub and a separate showering area. There were two different kinds of bubble bath sitting on the edge of the tub. One was vanilla and the other raspberry scent. The sink contained splashes of brown and green in the porcelain and the faucets were accented in gold. There was one toothbrush in the stainless steel toothbrush holder on the countertop.

Carmen switched off the bathroom light and proceeded down the hallway. The first room past the bathroom was a workout room. In one corner, there was a kicking bag and a speed bag. In the opposite corner was a set of weights, a chin-up bar, and an abdominal roller. Mirrors lined the far wall and a poster of Jean Claude Van Damme was taped to the back of the door.

Next to the workout room was the second bedroom that had been turned into an office. A large wooden bookshelf lined one side of the room and an executive-style mahogany desk with a computer and laser-jet printer occupied the other. Carmen walked over to the bookshelf and scanned the titles. There were various books on serial killers, forensic psychology, and the martial arts. She blushed when she noticed a book on lesbian sex on the bottom shelf. She pulled it out and began flipping through the pages.

Carmen had grown up in the Midwest where there had been many benefits growing up in a small town, but there had also been just as many drawbacks. One of the drawbacks was that there wasn't anyone to talk to if one chose to walk a path different from the norm. When Carmen realized that she judged people by what made them tick instead of basing her opinion on their race, color, gender, etc., she knew she was going to have an uphill battle. Things got worse when she realized that she was in love with her best friend, who happened to be a girl. She tried to confide her feelings in people whom she trusted, but they told her not to talk about such things. The bookstores in the area didn't carry anything even remotely related to lesbianism. So, she had to figure out quite a bit on her own.

Carmen continued to flip through the book until she came to a page showing different devices that could be used during sex. She quickly put the book back where she had found it and blushed. "Miss Childers," she whispered, "you are a naughty girl, aren't you?"

Carmen wandered back into the kitchen. She looked in the refrigerator for something to eat, but found Zoë was in desperate need of groceries. There were two diet sodas, a fourth of a gallon of milk, bacon, and some eggs that occupied the shelves. She grabbed one of the diet sodas and walked over to the portable telephone laying on the back edge of the couch. It was about 5:45 p.m. and she was starving. She picked up the phone and dialed information for the local pizza parlor. Once connected, she ordered breadsticks and a large pepperoni pizza for delivery. She placed the phone onto the floor and collapsed onto the plush couch pillows.

Carmen felt at home except for Cuffs not being with her. She allowed her eyelids to close and she drifted off to sleep within minutes. She awoke a short time later to the soft rhythmic knocking at the front door. She slowly pulled herself from the couch and looked at the clock on the wall. It had only been thirty-two minutes since she had ordered the pizza. She dug in her pockets for her money. "There is no way the pizza can be here already," she muttered under her breath. "It'll be raw."

She peered through the peephole and to her surprise Chris was standing on the front porch with a big bouquet of balloons and a teddy bear. The brightly colored red, yellow, green and blue balloons whipped wildly in the wind. The ribbons that were attached to the balloons were anchored to the fuzzy brown stuffed teddy bear sporting a deep purple bow tie. Carmen also noticed that Chris had a brown folder tightly wrapped with a green rubber band underneath his arm.

She unlocked the door and stepped back to let him in. She tried to look as deeply concerned as possible as she raised one eyebrow higher than the other. "Chris," she said solemnly, "does Mary know that you're bringing balloons over to another woman's house?"

"Well," he remarked, amused by Carmen's quick-witted humor, "she doesn't really mind all that much. It gives her time to let the mailman in."

Chris handed the bouquet of balloons to Carmen and kissed her on the check. He slipped off his loafers before any dirt could transfer onto the hardwood floors and set them just inside the doorway. Carmen set the teddy bear on the kitchen counter and searched the cabinets for some drinking glasses. She located them just to the left of the sink and fixed two ice-cold glasses of water. Chris took off his faded blue denim jacket and laid it across the back of the couch.

Just as Carmen and Chris settled themselves on opposite ends of the couch, the bedroom door opened and

Zoë stuck her head out. "I thought I heard a man's voice," she teased. "You're lucky I didn't just shoot your happy ass!"

"I'm a risk taker," Chris retorted.

Zoë winced with every step as she made her way over to the couch. She sat down on the rug in front of them. "Chris, you are such a sweetie," she said noticing the balloons. "Thank you so much! Please don't be offended if I don't get up right now to take a closer look."

"No problem at all and I do understand. Besides, I had to bring you a little something for saving my partner," Chris cooed, stretching his arms out in front of him. "Besides, I thought we should go over the case if you guys feel up to it."

The doorbell chimed again and Carmen strutted across the floor. She could feel Zoë's eyes follow her and she consciously tightened her butt muscles to make them look even firmer than they already were. She opened the door and a fair-haired boy about seventeen handed her a steaming hot pizza that warmed her hand. She gave him the money owed instructing him to keep the five dollars in change and closed the door. She sat the pizza with the bag of breadsticks on top of it next to Zoë and went into the kitchen.

"If you're looking for paper plates, there are some below the microwave," Zoë called after her.

• • •

The simple meal tasted like fine cuisine to Carmen and had she asked Chris and Zoë what they thought, they would have agreed. Zoë finished off her last piece of crust and tossed her napkin into the empty pizza box. Carmen picked up the box and threw it away along with the dirtied paper plates. She refilled each of their glasses with water and returned to the living room.

Chris flipped through the contents of the brown folder. He placed the crime scene photos on the coffee table and handed Carmen and Zoë copies of the case reports. Carmen skimmed the report and sighed dejectedly. The latent print examiner, Daniel, hadn't been able to locate a match for the fingerprint lifted off the mirror. The prints lifted from each of the knives left in the victims' hands belonged to the victims. The blood samples that were collected from both crime scenes had also been DNA typed back to the victims.

"Do either of you see anything to go on?" Chris questioned after about twenty minutes had passed.

"It says here," Carmen said, highlighting a paragraph of the report in yellow, "that the brown fibers found at the first victim's apartment were identified as carpet fibers."

"That's correct," Chris replied.

"So, let's think about this," Carmen suggested. "The fibers don't match any of the carpet samples that we collected from either crime scene."

"And," Zoë interjected, "the crime lab has determined that the fibers are commonly found in carpet designed for indoor or outdoor use."

"So, we're assuming the killer has indoor or outdoor carpeting at his home?" Chris questioned confused. "How does this help us?"

"I don't think it's at his home," Carmen said objectively. "I think it's in his van."

"We need to get a list of all utility van manufacturers that use this type of carpeting," Zoë remarked thoughtfully. "Then, we can start narrowing our search."

"I have to stop by the station on my way home anyway to give Cooper some study guides," Chris responded.

"So, I'll see if Debra is still around and if she can help us in gathering that information."

"Is Cooper thinking about taking the detective's exam?" Carmen asked.

"Yeah," Chris replied. "He really wants to work in homicide."

"Good for him," Zoë praised. "Now let's get back to the case."

"Alright, both women were killed by the same person," Carmen continued, "but there seems to be no other connection. Neither of the women knew one another nor had any mutual friends."

"So, what are we not seeing?" Zoë remarked looking over the report.

Carmen picked up the crime scene photos and shuffled through them. She set two pictures aside and placed the rest back down on the coffee table. She studied the two pictures for a few moments. "Take a look at these," she urged. "Can you see what I'm seeing?"

Chris accepted the two photos and examined each one closely. He shrugged his shoulders and handed them off to Zoë. "These aren't even pictures of the rooms where the victims were found," he stated. "What do their living rooms have to do with anything?"

Carmen took the two pictures from Zoë and tried to refrain from sounding too cocky. "Chris, let me ask you something," she began. "What does your wife like to get for no reason at all?"

"Cards and chocolate," he answered. "Unless, I've really screwed up then she wants flowers and diamonds."

"No way!" Zoë exclaimed, snatching the pictures back from Carmen's hands. "Both photos have fresh flowers in them!"

"I would bet that our suspect is disguising himself as just a regular good guy just wanting to take these women out or as a flower delivery man. The women let him in because they either recognize him or don't feel threatened."

"Damn Carmen, people should shoot at you more often," Chris said chuckling. "You become smarter every time! I'll go get the vases in the morning and put them into evidence. Hopefully, there will be some prints that Daniel can work with. At least we have a little bit more to go on." Chris gathered up all the paperwork and placed it back into the folder. "Will you need a ride home tonight?"

"No thanks," Carmen attempted, her usual quick thinking failing her miserably as she tried to conjure up a reason to convince her partner that she needed to stay.

"If she doesn't mind," Zoë interjected, "I need help changing the bandages on my shoulder. She can stay on the couch tonight if doesn't want to call a cab."

"I think that's a great idea," Chris mused, leaning over and giving Zoë a quick peck on the cheek. "You just take care of yourself, okay?"

"I plan on it and thanks again for the balloons and teddy bear."

"You're welcome."

Carmen escorted Chris out to his car. The sun was beginning to set over the western horizon withdrawing its warm rays of light. "Be extra careful," she warned hugging him tightly. "He came after me, who's to say he won't come after you?"

Chris kissed her forehead and smiled. "Don't worry about me little lady," he said in a southern drawl. "I have a patrol car keeping an eye on my house."

"Good thinking."

"I also have another one keeping an eye on the two of you," he revealed with an ornery grin pointing discreetly down the road. "So, don't be doing anything that I wouldn't do."

"Thanks Chris," she said, ignoring his comment and glancing at the unmarked police car not more than two blocks away. "You're always there for me, aren't you?"

"Well, I try to be. Besides, no one else can put up with my shit as well as you can."

"Well, no one else would put up with my crap either," she laughed. "Take care of yourself and I'll call you tomorrow."

Chris buckled himself in and shut the driver's side door. He rolled down the window and peered up at her with a mischievous grin. "Carmen," he began, "you do know that people who have been in accidents shouldn't have any sort of rough housing, right?"

Taken off guard by the comment, she was immediately embarrassed. Speechless, she just stood there as Chris rolled up his window, smiled wickedly, and drove away.

• • •

Carmen double-checked the front door to make sure she locked it and immediately noticed that Zoë was no longer in the living room. She headed for the bedroom genuinely concerned that something might be wrong. When she peeked into the darkened room, she felt a slight rush of panic at the sight of the empty bed. She placed her hand on the Glock still tucked into the waist of her jeans. "Zoë?" she called out. "Where are you?"

"I'm in the bathroom," Zoë cried out. "I'm just a little sick. I'll be okay in just a minute."

Compelled to be at her side, Carmen hurried into the bathroom. Zoë was resting her forehead on the outside rim of the toilet. "Please, Carmen, I don't want you to see me like this," she pleaded, her face pallid.

Carmen rushed over as Zoë began throwing up again. She pulled Zoë's hair back away from her face and rubbed the small of her back. After a few minutes, Zoë sat back totally exhausted. Carmen took the opportunity to search the bathroom sink cabinet for a small hand towel or washcloth. Finding a small towel, Carmen soaked it with cold water and patted the back of Zoë's neck with it.

"I'm sorry you have to see me like this," Zoë stated wearily. "It's not exactly what I had planned for tonight."

"I wouldn't want to be anywhere else than with you," Carmen assured.

"You're so sweet."

"Now, enough talk, let's get you into bed," Carmen insisted, helping Zoë to her feet.

Zoë brushed her teeth and washed her face before following Carmen into the bedroom. She climbed into bed and dragged herself over to one side. She hadn't realized how exhausted she had become until she attempted to unbutton her jeans. Unable to muster up any more energy, she gazed up at Carmen in defeat, "Will you please help me get these off?"

"Sure, honey."

Carmen knelt down beside Zoë and unzipped her jeans. She pulled them from her hips and over the muscular curves of her legs. She tossed them onto the floor and tried not to stare at the silky blue bikini underwear that Zoë was wearing. Desire surged through her body and relinquished her lips and mouth of any moisture. She couldn't resist taking one last look before pulling the top sheet up around Zoë.

"You are so beautiful," Zoë mumbled struggling to keep her eyes open. "Please forgive me for being so ill."

Touched, Carmen ran her fingers through Zoë's hair. "You saved my life," she reminded her softly. "I'm the one who's sorry that you're not feeling well."

Zoë gave her a weary smile and closed her eyes. "If you want to," she murmured, "you can sleep in here with me instead of the couch. I don't think I kick."

"Alright," Carmen whispered kissing Zoë's brow. "I'll be back in just a minute."

Carmen tiptoed out of the bedroom and quickly made her way through the living room. She verified one last time that the front door was locked before heading to the bathroom to wash her face. When she finished drying her hands, Carmen plugged in the nightlight that was resting on the back of the toilet and turned off all the lights. She went back to the bedroom and pulled the red oriental blanket up around Zoë's shoulders. She moved to the other side of the bed and slipped off her jeans and socks. She eased in between the sheets and switched off the small ceramic lamp sitting on the nightstand next to her. She could hear Zoë's soft rhythmic breathing and feel her body heat warming the bed.

* * *

Zoë awakened about 2 a.m. to find Carmen crying in her sleep. She pulled Carmen close and whispered comfortingly, "Its okay, honey. I'll never let anything happen to you. I've got you, baby." Carmen eventually fell silent, but Zoë stayed awake for a long time afterward, holding her and running her fingers through her soft blond hair.

Around 8:30 a.m., Carmen awoke refreshed and surprised to find herself in Zoë's arms. She was careful not to wake Zoë as she rose up onto her elbow. It had been a long time since Carmen had woken up with anyone, and this wasn't just anyone, this was her dream girl. So before she really thought about it, she began lightly touching the side of Zoë's cheek and tracing her jaw line with her fingertips. She ran her hand through Zoë's dark brown hair before moving down to her shoulders.

Carmen glided her hand over the silkiness of Zoë's shirt feeling the firmness of her breasts and the ripples of Zoë's washboard stomach. Then, by accident, she brushed her hand against the silky bikini underwear that impeded her ability to view Zoë's sweet succulent valley. She couldn't resist running her fingertip along the top seam. She smiled when she encountered a small tuff of wavy hair peeking out the top. She traced around Zoë's pelvic bone and along the inside of her thigh where the temperature seemed to be scorching. Shyly, she pulled her hand away, but found that she wanted more. It had been a long time since she had touched another woman, much less had one touch her.

Carmen's last lover had decided one night that she wanted out. Carmen had been so stunned that she blamed herself and fought to get her back. Unfortunately, she found out later that her ex had been seeing someone for the four months prior to them breaking up. Two years later, her ex had wanted to come back, but Carmen just couldn't let her into her heart again after all that had happened. Carmen also knew that she harbored feelings for Zoë. But at the time, she had been informed that Miss Zoë Childers was a heartbreak waiting to happen. So, her innocent infatuation would never amount to much.

Absorbed in her thoughts, Carmen hadn't notice that Zoë's breathing had changed. Carmen ran her fingertips along the top seam of Zoë's underwear once again before slipping them beneath the silky barrier. Her mouth went dry as she found her fingers entwined among the delicate hairs of Zoë's private garden. She bent down and grasped Zoë's t-shirt with her teeth and pulled it upward just enough to begin lightly kissing her stomach. She felt Zoë's body quiver and the realization it brought began sinking in. She bowed her head and pulled her hand away. She could sense Zoë's beautiful green eyes staring at her. Zoë cupped Carmen's chin and lifted it upward until their eyes met.

"I'm so sorry!" Carmen cried out. "It's just that since the first day I met you, I've wanted to know what it would be like to wake up with you."

Zoë pulled her arm out from underneath Carmen and painfully turned over onto her side so that they were face to face. She could see the panic in Carmen's eyes. She knew that mere words would not do at a moment like this. So, she leaned forward and kissed Carmen passionately.

"My God," Carmen breathed as their lips parted.

"I don't know why you're apologizing to me," Zoë stated softly, "I like you being here when I wake up too."

With that, Zoë kissed Carmen again so passionately that Carmen's body visibly trembled. Carmen's hips surged upward as Zoë carefully lay down on top of her. Zoë moved her lips to Carmen's earlobes and down her neck. She continued to kiss her until the material of Carmen's shirt was the only thing between her mouth and Carmen's hardened nipples. She bit down on Carmen's shirt and grasped it between her teeth. She gingerly shook her head from side to side with the shirt still secured in her mouth. Her eyes locked in on Carmen's.

Carmen knew what Zoë wanted and she removed her shirt. As soon as her breasts were uncovered, Zoë's hot passionate lips were kissing them, her tongue dancing softly on each nipple causing them to ache with pleasure.

Zoë continued her downward descent and kissed every inch of Carmen's stomach. She wanted to memorize every freckle, mark, and scar that graced her delicate skin. She traced Carmen's belly button with her tongue and tantalized it with quick strokes symbolizing what she was intending to do. She could feel Carmen's hands starting to claw at her back in desire-filled aggression.

Carmen ran her hands up to Zoë's head and gently pushed her toward the one area few had been allowed to visit. Her body screamed for release and she was suddenly aware of how extremely moist she was. "Zoë, I want you," she gasped maneuvering her hips away from Zoë's face. "As God as my witness, I want you. It's just. . ."

Zoë immediately lifted her eyes to meet Carmen's. "I'm moving too fast, aren't I?" she interjected, her voice filled with anguish. "I just thought that this was what you wanted."

"It's not you. It's me. I'm starting to care a lot about you," Carmen insisted truthfully. "I haven't made love with anyone in a long time and I'm really. . ." Carmen looked at Zoë with the most sheepish eyes possible and breathed her last word, "wet."

An understanding smile touched the corners of Zoë's mouth. She moved carefully up Carmen's body attempting to protect her right shoulder from any unintentional encounter with pain. She could feel Carmen trembling as she laid down next to her. She brushed back Carmen's soft blonde hair and stared lovingly into her eyes. "Trust me honey," Zoë encouraged.

"I do," Carmen answered defenselessly.

Zoë glided her hand down the front Carmen's slender physique and continuously kissed her lips. When her fingers touched the top of Carmen's cotton underwear, Zoë slipped them underneath the fabric and her fingers were immediately dampened. A surge of desire flashed through her. She could not resist following the trail of warmth.

Carmen gave a soft cry of delight as Zoë's fingers slipped inside of her. Their kisses instantly became more passionate as their bodies rocked in harmony with one another. Zoë used the strength in her hands to pulse inside of Carmen causing the sensational ache of an orgasm to build. Carmen grabbed hold of Zoë's ribcage and bit down softly on her bottom lip. She stifled a scream of ecstasy as her body exploded in waves of climatic pleasure. Zoë continued to kiss her neck and nibble on her ears until her body stilled.

Carmen lay breathless. She could feel Zoë's fingers moving gingerly back and forth inside of her. Although, she was more then willing to have Zoë take her that way again, she had never experienced love making with another woman like that before. Her body was still trembling from the power of the last orgasm. "Zoë, I'm not sure if I can handle that right now," she gasped.

Zoë moved directly down to where her hand had been and peeled off Carmen's underwear. She kissed Carmen's inner thighs and managed to move Carmen's quivering legs further apart. Slowly, she removed her hand and offered soft strokes of her tongue in its place. She indulged in the sweet tastes cascading into her mouth as she explored every last intimate area with her tongue.

Carmen closed her eyes and could not resist letting all her reservations go. She felt safe with Zoë. She had never had anyone take such time in discovering her body. She felt Zoë's fingers inside of her again while her tongue, still strong with desire, pulsated against her clitoris. Her thighs began to quiver, her back arched, and her hands were in Zoë's hair pressing Zoë against her hips.

"Oh God!" Carmen moaned, her voice strained, but growing louder as the intensity overwhelmed her. "Please, Zoë, don't stop!"

Carmen found herself teetering on the edge of release. She bit down on the satiny pillow that her head was resting on. She wrapped her legs around Zoë's lower back and pressed her hips upward. She squeezed her eyes closed as she welcomed another tidal wave of orgasmic release.

Zoë lapped up the exquisite sweetness that poured into her mouth. When Carmen's body ceased quivering, Zoë conjured up enough strength to move her extremely sore shoulder and aching body back up beside Carmen. She pulled Carmen into her arms and stroked her hair. Before long, Carmen fell asleep and Zoë could feel Carmen's hot breath fall rhythmically on her chest.

Zoë felt at peace with Carmen beside her. "I would be completely content spending the rest of my life loving you," she whispered.

CHAPTER SEVEN

A phone rang in the distance and Carmen forced her eyes open. She rose up onto her elbows and looked around trying to get her bearings. She immediately noticed that she was in bed alone. She jumped up, slipped on her underwear, and grabbed her shirt pulling it over her head as she opened the bedroom door. She hoped that Zoë wasn't sick again.

When Carmen entered the living room, she saw Zoë in the kitchen. Zoë was holding the cordless telephone between her ear and left shoulder as she scrambled some eggs in a skillet. Carmen cringed at the loving way that Zoë spoke to whoever was on the other end of the phone. Jealousy surged through Carmen's veins like a street drug in the purest form. She quietly crept into the kitchen to hear what was being said.

Zoë didn't see Carmen approach. As fate would have it, she turned around and jumped back in total surprise. She slammed her right shoulder into the cabinet door that was still left open. "Holy shit!" Zoë cried out in pain.

"I'm so sorry," Carmen gasped not knowing what else to do.

"Mom, I'm okay," Zoë said reassuringly into the receiver. "Everything's okay. The woman I've been telling you about. . . Yes, the detective."

Zoë fell silent and Carmen could hear Zoë's mom getting onto her about something. Finally, Zoë sighed and was obviously biting her tongue as she spoke. "Mom, I think I'm old enough to let whomever I want stay the night and take care of me," she retorted. "Anyway back to the point, she startled me and I bumped my shoulder. It's no big deal."

Carmen felt horrible. How could she have thought that someone as wonderful as Zoë would be talking to anyone else besides her mother in such a loving way? She could see the immense pain in Zoë's eyes as she tried to rub the soreness from her shoulder with her other hand. "I'm really sorry," Carmen mouthed resisting the roaring rollercoaster of guilt that seemed to be twisting around in her gut.

Zoë gave Carmen a wink and pushed a plateful of sizzling bacon and steaming scrabbled eggs over to her. "I love you too, Mom," she stated. "Please tell Linda to stop worrying about me."

Carmen accepted the plate and walked over to the couch. She sat down with her legs tucked up underneath her and placed the plate of food in her lap. Zoë hung up the phone and made her way into the living room. She wasn't sure where she stood in the grand scheme of things so she resisted placing her hand on Carmen's thigh as she sat down next to her.

Zoë studied Carmen's facial expression. She was terrified Carmen might think she had made a terrible mistake earlier and leave at any time. Finally, Zoë summoned up enough courage to break the silence. "Chris called earlier and said you were ordered to take today off," she informed nervously.

"That's great," Carmen replied without a smidge of emotion.

"But, I guess your Captain said that you have to be back tomorrow," Zoë continued.

"That's very considerate of Captain Zebrowski," Carmen remarked sarcastically.

"I heard he's a jerk," Zoë responded.

"You heard right," Carmen replied.

"Before I forget," Zoë added. "Chris also wanted me to tell you that Cuffs is fine and that he would call back later."

"Thanks."

"Did I do something wrong?" Zoë prodded, bracing for the worst.

"Not at all," Carmen answered slightly confused. "I was the one that did something wrong."

"What did you do?" Zoë asked bewildered.

"I startled you while you were on the phone," Carmen said without looking up. "I heard you talking and I thought. . ."

"You thought I was talking to another woman, right?" Zoë interrupted.

"Yeah, how did you know that's what I was going to say?" Carmen responded surprised.

"The look on your face was a dead give away," Zoë responded with a genuine laugh. "Besides, women know these things, don't they?"

"I guess we do," Carmen agreed relieved. "So, you're not mad at me for causing you to hit your shoulder?"

"Mad?" Zoë said quizzically. "No, I'm not mad at all. In fact, I'm flattered. I just wish flattery didn't have to hurt so much."

They both laughed. "You're still not feeling well are you?" Carmen asked, noticing Zoë's face was a little pale and she wasn't eating.

"Well, I just thought it better that I didn't eat too much today in order to give my stomach a rest," Zoë replied cheerfully.

"So, how's your shoulder feeling?" Carmen prodded, her cheeks reddening slightly.

"It was a little sore from this morning," Zoë replied shyly. "I took a pain pill just before I started cooking breakfast, just in case I did anything else that might aggravate it."

Carmen's thoughts raced back to their early morning escapade. She knew she was glowing and what she felt for Zoë was so unmistakable that she wanted to scream it from the tallest building in the city. Zoë had stolen her heart and made love to her in a way that no one else ever had. She needed to be with Zoë again. She needed to make love to Zoë, to touch her, caress her, and love her just as she had been made love with.

Zoë had been silently watching her, "Carmen, are you alright?"

"I'm fine. I was just thinking," she replied. "Do you have any plans for today?"

"Well, I'm going to go change these bandages." Zoë replied hesitantly. "And, spend the rest of the day with you, if that's alright?"

"Yeah, I would love that. I'll put this dish away and then help you change your bandages," Carmen responded enthusiastically. "I'll be just a minute."

• • •

Zoë stripped off her clothes and placed an oversized white fluffy towel around her body. She peeled off the bandages from her right shoulder as Carmen entered the bathroom. "I thought I would take a shower first," she declared.

"That's a good idea," Carmen replied. "It'll probably make you feel better."

"Would you mind helping me wrap my shoulder with saran wrap?"

"Sure, just tell me where it is."

Carmen found the saran wrap in the exact kitchen drawer Zoë said it would be in. She hurried back to the bathroom with the entire roll. Zoë had adjusted the towel so that it only covered her waist. Carmen struggled not to blatantly stare as she wrapped Zoë's shoulder. As Carmen finished, Zoë turned to face her, "Would you like to take a shower with me?"

Carmen's tongue ceased functioning for a moment and all she could do was nod her head. Zoë turned on the shower and kept checking the water for warmth. Neither of them spoke as if saying something might allow the moment to escape into the steam fogging up the mirror. Finally, Zoë smiled shyly, dropped the towel onto the floor, and quickly stepped into the shower.

A million thoughts raced through Carmen's mind. She had only taken a shower with one other person. Zoë would see her completely naked without a blanket or sheet to escape under when she got shy. Then, a wonderful thought occurred to Carmen. She would be able to see all of Zoë as well. With that notion, she took off her shirt and cotton underwear and slipped into the steamy shower.

Zoë indulged herself beneath the warm water spraying from the shower nozzle. Streams of water poured over her thick satiny hair pooling at the base and plummeting down her V-shaped back. Carmen followed the water's path as it descended down over Zoë's butt and the muscular curves of her legs. Zoë turned around and bent her head back into the water. Carmen followed another stream of water as it cascaded over Zoë's breasts and onto her rippled stomach before disappearing into the secret garden that she so wanted to explore.

"You are even more beautiful than I imagined," Carmen breathed.

"Thank you."

As Zoë began fidgeting with the shampoo bottle, Carmen realized that it was quite possible that Zoë was just as shy about taking a shower with someone as she was. So, she wrapped her arms around Zoë's waist and laid her head against Zoë's chest. She could feel Zoë trembling even though the water falling down on them was still pleasantly warm. Carmen looked up into Zoë's green eyes and unconsciously moistened her lips.

Zoë wrapped her arms around Carmen and kissed her tenderly. When the water temperature dropped a degree or so in warmth, Zoë grabbed the bar of soap off the built in shelf and began washing Carmen's body. Carmen, captivated by this advance, stood helplessly, falling deeper and deeper in love. The water could have been freezing and she would have never noticed.

Zoë first washed Carmen's face, then her neck and shoulders. She soaped up Carmen's chest and lingered for a little while as she massaged her breasts enjoying the hardness that developed in Carmen's nipples. Zoë dropped to her knees and lathered up Carmen's stomach and thighs. She washed between Carmen's legs and felt the warm moisture pool in her hand.

Upon Zoë's request, Carmen rinsed the soap off her body and turned around. Zoë poured a small amount of shampoo into her hand and massaged it into Carmen's scalp.

Carmen arched her head back and allowed the cool spray of water to rinse out the shampoo. Then, Zoë squeezed a little bit of conditioner on top of Carmen's head and worked it through before adding a little more to the baby fine ends.

Carmen leaned back into the spray. She ran her fingers one more time through her hair to make sure all the conditioner was out. She quivered when she felt Zoë's warm lips kissing her stomach. She placed her hand against the shower wall for added support as Zoë's tongue traced her pelvic bone. Before long, she was against the shower wall with Zoë's face buried into her wetness. She was barely touching the floor of the shower and her legs were tingling from the intensity of the strokes from Zoë's tongue. Her thighs tightened and with a sudden release, she flooded into Zoë's wanting mouth.

Zoë placed her left arm around Carmen to hold her up and kissed her passionately. The water was now lukewarm and Zoë cupped Carmen's face and looked deep into her eyes. "I want you to dry off and climb back into bed," she ordered. "I'll finish my shower before the water becomes too frigid. Then, I'll come hold you if you want me to."

"I would love that," Carmen stated exhaustedly. She stepped out of the shower and pulled a towel from the rack. She dried off quickly and slipped her t-shirt back on. She wiped the steam from the mirror and stared at her reflection. She couldn't stop herself from asking the question that had been demanding to be voiced from the back of her mind. "Zoë, how long has it been?" she inquired softly.

Zoë peeked from around the curtain, her hair lathered with shampoo, "How long has it been since what?"

Amused by Zoë's attempt to play dumb, Carmen elaborated, "I mean, I know that rumor has it that you are a real heartbreaker."

"Well, I don't think rumors are much to invest in, do you?" Zoë remarked bluntly, disappearing behind the curtain.

"So, if you don't mind me asking," Carmen pressed, not satisfied with Zoë's response. "When was the last time you had someone in your bed? Yesterday, last week, last month, last year? I just want to know if I have any competition."

Zoë did not respond and the unexpected silence seemed to drown out the sounds of the shower. Carmen knew she had unintentionally struck a nerve. Zoë turned off the shower and reached out yanking the other towel off the towel rack. She disappeared behind the curtain for a moment and then stepped out of the shower with the towel wrapped around her. Carmen noticed that Zoë wouldn't even look at her.

"I'm sorry," Carmen offered, terrified that she had blown her chance with having anything serious with Zoë. "You don't have to tell me."

"About 4 or 5 years ago, okay?" Zoë remarked almost hatefully. "Since then, I haven't wanted to be close to another woman or remember the last time I allowed a woman to be in bed with me. Why? Do you think the rumors are true, Detective Moore? Do you actually believe I sleep around?"

If Carmen hadn't noticed that Zoë was close to tears, she would have started crying herself. But, as she looked at Zoë, she saw the regret filtering into her eyes. She knew Zoë's anger was not meant for her. "No," Carmen uttered, her voice cracking slightly, "I don't believe the rumors are true."

"Carmen," Zoë pleaded, realizing what an asshole she had just been. "I'm so sorry for lashing out at you like that." Tears raced down Zoë's strong cheekbones. "Please don't hold that against me," she begged.

Carmen took Zoë by the hand and grabbed the bandages off the bathroom counter. She led Zoë to the bedroom and over to the bed. "Why don't you sit down," Carmen suggested patting the edge of the bed. "It'll be easier to doctor you up that way."

"Sure," Zoë said weakly as she complied with Carmen's request.

Carmen removed the saran wrap and scrunched it up into a small ball before tossing it into the silver waste basket next to the nightstand. She patted the area dry and squeezed a small amount of antibiotic onto Zoë's shoulder. She rubbed the cream around the stitches and placed a couple of gauze pads over it before bandaging it up. She threw out the sterile wrappers that the gauze and bandages had been packaged in and squatted down in front of Zoë. "I wasn't trying to pry," she offered taking Zoë's hands into her own.

"Carmen, I haven't wanted to be with anyone for a long time," Zoë revealed. "I thought I had found someone to spend my life with about five years ago. Her name was Kristin and I really wanted to settle down with her. One night, I decided to tell her that I loved her and that I wanted to spend my life with her. Apparently, she just wanted a relationship with no commitment. The next night when I was at work, she just up and left and I haven't heard from her since."

Carmen could not believe that anyone would want to leave such a wonderful woman. What words could she say to this confession? She needed to comfort Zoë, but that would mean re-opening a wound that she had forced herself to close. "I haven't been with anyone in about three and half years," she offered finally. "My ex, Laura, left me because my job took me away so much."

"What do you mean?" Zoë inquired. "She had to know how much you wanted to be a detective."

"Well, one day when I got home from work everything was gone except for Cuffs. Laura left a note saying that she needed to find a woman who loved her more than a job. I never thought I would ever get over that, especially when I found out she had been seeing someone else for about four months."

"That's harsh," Zoë interjected.

"And, the thing was that I didn't love my job more than I loved her. I wanted to do the best job I could because of her."

"I'm sorry," Zoë whispered squeezing Carmen's hands. "Laura was an idiot to ever leave you. I know I would never leave you."

Zoë began to rub her shoulder in an attempt to hide the honesty of her last statement. Carmen, surprised and touched by her remark, softly touched Zoë's face. "Why don't you rest for a minute?" Carmen suggested, motioning Zoë to lay her head on the satiny pillow.

Zoë removed the towel from her waist and pulled the covers up around her chest as she lay back on the pillow. "It's a little chilly in here," she whispered.

"You won't be cold long," Carmen stated.

Carmen removed her shirt and slipped in between the sheets. She felt Zoë's body tense as she nestled up beside her. She caught Zoë's gaze and curled her fingers around locks of her hair. "May I touch you?" Carmen asked, her voice thick with desire.

"Yes," Zoë replied nervously.

Carmen leaned forward and kissed across Zoë's brow, down her nose, and onto her lips. She made sure not to bump Zoë's shoulder as she moved gingerly on top of her. They continuously kissed and Carmen caressed Zoë's breasts enjoying the billowy softness in her hands. She ran her fingertips over the ripples of Zoë's stomach and the curves of her hips. She felt the smoothness and strength of her legs.

Unable to resist, Carmen brought her hand steadily back up Zoë's thigh and slipped her fingers between Zoë's legs. Instantly, Zoë pleaded in desperation, "Please, I need to hold you."

"You will have plenty of time to hold me," Carmen replied, "after I make love with you."

"But," Zoë began to argue.

"I won't up and leave you," Carmen promised. "Trust me."

Carmen slipped her fingers past the gates of Zoë's private oasis and penetrated the entrance that led into her beautiful body. Her fingers explored this inner sanctuary as Zoë's hips rocked gently upward. Carmen searched passionately for the spot that would invoke an unequivocal orgasm. When she felt the muscles surrounding her fingers tighten, she knew she had found it.

Zoë grabbed a hold of Carmen's back with one hand. "Don't stop," she pleaded.

"I won't stop," Carmen assured.

Zoë felt Carmen's fingers pulsate even faster inside of her. The rise to orgasmic release was sweet and long overdue. The muscles in her legs and butt tightened. The moisture in her mouth evaporated. She arched her head back and squeezed her eyes shut. Her hips surged upward as her body screamed to feel more of Carmen inside of her.

As if reading her mind, Carmen slipped another finger inside of her. "Oh, God!" Zoë gasped burying her face into Carmen's shoulder. Zoë tried to stifle another cry of sheer pleasure, but couldn't. "Oh, my God!" she screamed again as her body erupted in intense orgasmic shudders.

Carmen felt the warm nectar that enveloped her hand and she couldn't resist any longer. She moved gracefully down

Zoë's body kissing and caressing every inch. She lingered at her breasts taking each nipple into her mouth. She kissed her stomach and stroked Zoë's pelvic bone with her tongue. She nibbled on the inside of Zoë's thighs breathing in the scent that she so wanted to taste.

"I don't think I have ever. . ." Zoë whispered. "It was so amazing."

"I need to taste you," Carmen declared before burying her face between Zoë's legs.

Zoë clenched the satiny bed sheets in her hand. Her inner thighs trembled from Carmen's soft tongue strokes. She could feel her orgasm building, intensifying, and stealing energy from her head to her toes. Before she realized it, she was begging Carmen once again. "Please! Oh God," she gasped. "Please don't stop!" Zoë grabbed the back of Carmen's head pressing Carmen's tongue deeper inside of her. She screamed out Carmen's name before all communication stilled. The power of her orgasm stole her breath and she lay gasping as Carmen drank her sweet nectar.

• • •

Zoë nuzzled her head against Carmen's breast. "You're amazing," she whispered.

"I'm not amazing," Carmen stated as she stroked Zoë's hair. "You are amazing."

"Well," Zoë replied sleepily, "I know I'm the lucky one."

With that, Zoë fell asleep. Carmen watched the time pass on the digital clock that glowed from the nightstand for about fifteen minutes. She called out Zoë's name a couple times to make sure that she was asleep. Confidant that Zoë was in fact sleeping, Carmen confided what she felt in her heart, "I love you, Zoë Childers."

Fighting back tears of joy, Zoë did not attempt to spoil the moment. She closed her eyes again and listened to the beating of Carmen's heart.

CHAPTER EIGHT

Carmen didn't notice Chris staring at her from his desk. In fact, at the present moment, she was hardly aware she was at the police station at all. She was reliving the passion she and Zoë shared over the past two days in her mind. The unexpected ring of her desk phone snapped her back into reality. She fumbled for the receiver managing somehow to not knock it off the desk. "Hello?" she greeted exasperated.

"I was just wondering what or who has you so distracted," the male caller inquired.

The deep voice could only belong to one person. Carmen could sense him watching her. She gazed across the room at Chris kicked back in his chair with his brown suede loafers up on his desk. He dropped the telephone receiver onto its cradle and smirked.

"You are such a pain in the ass," she hollered slamming the phone down.

Chris stood up and tried to smooth out the creases that were forming in his slacks. He tucked his hands into his pockets and casually walked toward Carmen's desk. As he opened his mouth to respond to Carmen's remark, her desk phone rang again. Carmen eyed him wickedly and grabbed the receiver, "Detective Moore, may I help you?"

"Detective Moore," the terrified voice squeaked, "that van is back."

Carmen recognized Natalie's voice immediately. "Are you sure?" Carmen questioned, looking up at Chris and switching over to speakerphone. "Are you sure it's the same van?"

"I am absolutely positive," Natalie vowed. "The driver is standing beside Ms. Lopez's car looking toward my house."

"Everything's going to be just fine," Carmen said calmly.

"What do I do?" Natalie demanded, her voice almost at a whisper.

"Chris and I are on our way," Carmen stated getting to her feet. "Lock all the doors and don't let him in if he should come over for any reason, okay?"

"Hurry, Detective Moore," Natalie's frightened little voice insisted. "Please hurry!"

"I want you to call 9-1-1 and keep our dispatch informed on what he's doing, okay?" Carmen instructed. "It won't take us long to get there, I promise."

"Okay," Natalie replied. "But, I'm so scared."

"It'll be alright."

"You promise?"

"I promise," Carmen reiterated. "Now, hang up and call 9-1-1."

"Bye," Natalie stated before quickly hanging up the phone.

Carmen grabbed her jacket off the back of the chair and raced after Chris. Her mind was racing as she ran through the police parking lot. Why did he go back? Does he think someone saw him? Did he lose something?

Carmen jumped into the passenger seat of Chris' unmarked car. Neither she nor Chris spoke as he eased the sedan out onto the main thoroughfare and turned right heading for the highway on-ramp. He flipped a switch on the console and the flashing red and blue lights mounted in the windshield were illuminated. They exited the highway and traveled about four miles south to the expansive housing subdivision in which Natalie lived.

Chris eased into the turn lane as the crackle of the police radio interrupted the silence. "Unit 24, the suspect is leaving the area," the dispatcher announced.

Carmen and Chris looked down the road that they were about to turn on. A brown van barreled toward the intersection with no apparent intention of stopping. The van attempted to turn right around the corner and fishtailed. Carmen braced herself for impact as the van skidded toward them. Within mere inches of smashing into the side of Chris' sedan, the driver of the van managed to regain control of the vehicle and continue down the road with increasing speed. Chris punched the accelerator and left deep rubber imprints on the roadway as he made a u-turn. The chase was on.

● ● ●

Trying to keep up with the van wouldn't have been a problem, but the driver's erratic lane changes, excessive speed, and total disregard of all traffic laws were causing mayhem on the streets of Elan. Chris maintained a close distance but left room to maneuver if he had too. Carmen was in constant communication with dispatch informing them on their changing locations. She could hear the sirens from other squad cars in the distance, but none had been able to catch up yet.

"I need you to get closer," Carmen demanded. "I can't see the license plate numbers."

Without warning, a gunshot sounded, then another and another. Chris swerved violently as one of the shots embedded itself into the grill of his car. "Son of a bitch!" he yelled angrily, trying to maintain control, but it was too late. The unmarked sedan left the roadway and plunged over a steep embankment.

• • •

The front end of the unmarked sedan was crunched into the engine compartment from the sudden impact with the embankment. Radiator fluid spilled all over the hot engine saturating the air with a foul stench. Dark plumes of smoke drifted up into the cloudless deep blue sky. The front two tires were flat and the rims bent inward. Chris paced back and forth as he studied the damage to his car.

Sweat beads ran down the bridge of Carmen's nose and dripped down onto the sizzling pavement. Her silk shirt was sticking to her hot skin. The bluish-green bruise forming on the front of her left shin ached. Her head and neck felt like she had been at a rock concert all night, head-banging to incomprehensible music. Even so, she refused to allow the crowd that had gathered around the accident to see her in pain.

"What was he doing there?" Chris stammered repeatedly, not caring who was in earshot. "We went over that place a hundred times! There's nothing there!"

"Well, apparently we've missed something," Carmen replied evenly.

"We didn't miss anything."

"Did you notice how he handled that van?" Carmen remarked not wanting to embark on this rampage with Chris.

"Yeah, he handled it a little too well," he contemplated aloud. "It was almost like he had some prior training in emergency vehicle operations."

"Maybe he did," Carmen reasoned.

Chris kicked the rear driver's side tire in disgust, "Do you think we could be dealing with an ex-cop or something?"

"It's a possibility," Carmen replied. "What I do know is that we need to go over the evidence again. We've missed something and this guy is really starting to piss me off always being a step ahead of us."

• • •

Two hours later, Chris and Carmen pulled up in front of the Mexican hacienda in a borrowed police cruiser. Officer Adrian McCoy's squad car was parked in Natalie's driveway. Adrian and Natalie were sitting on the front porch talking and greeted them with a wave. Carmen waved back as she closed the passenger side door.

For an hour and a half, Carmen and Chris went over every inch of the crime scene. They searched through the trash cans and the kitchen cabinets. They re-examined the dining room and living room. They inspected the two bathrooms and both bedrooms. Disappointed, they gave up, sweaty and defeated.

Adrian was leaning against the borrowed squad car when Chris and Carmen emerged from the crime scene. She was 5'11" and looked astonishing in uniform. Her short red hair was flared out at the ends and the mirrored sunglasses that she wore hid her caring, ocean blue eyes. Carmen knew that Adrian rarely allowed her true personality to show anyway. She had to put up with a lot of crap from the other officers on her shift. It wasn't just because she was a woman that they gave her a hard time, but because of a tragic incident that occurred years before.

During Adrian's first year as an officer, her partner was shot as he approached what appeared to be an abandoned vehicle. As fate would have it, the vehicle was actually stolen and the guy who stole it was lying in the front seat. When Adrian's partner shined his light through the driver's side window, the thief shot him at point blank range in the chest. But, what the car thief failed to see was that Adrian had stepped up next to the passenger side window of the vehicle a split second later. She fired four rounds into the car, killing the suspect. When backup arrived, they found Adrian holding her partner in her arms. Without a bulletproof vest on, he never had a chance. He was pronounced dead at the scene.

Carmen remembered how the guys used to tease Adrian and say things like, "Don't be her partner, she'll get you killed." Even though this was their way of dealing with a terrible tragedy, it caused Adrian severe heartache. Carmen had never seen Adrian cry over the incident. Then, one day one of the officers began shooting off his mouth and brought the incident up again. He lashed out at Adrian and stated that a woman had no right to be on the force because it endangered all the other officers. Infuriated, Adrian punched him right in the nose and walked out of the room.

Carmen had followed her and found her in the locker room crying. She comforted Adrian and took her to dinner after work that night. Adrian asked Carmen to spend the night with her and Carmen accepted. They spent most of the night talking about the terrible night that Adrian's partner had been killed. Then, Carmen stroked her hair until she fell asleep. Nothing physical ever happened between them, but a special bond had formed. Since then, she and Adrian had become good friends.

"Well, if it isn't my favorite detective and her sidekick, Tonto," Adrian teased slightly out of character.

"Hey! When did I become a sidekick?" Chris playfully whined. "Last time I checked I was the Lone Ranger!"

"That was before you got married," Carmen interjected. "Now, you're controlled by two women, one at home and one at work."

"Just give it up," Adrian chimed in. "Women dominate your life."

"I just let my wife and my partner think that they have the upper hand, but we all know who wears the pants in both relationships," Chris responded, puffing out his chest and nodding his head with self-mocking admiration.

"Well, I think I have had enough testosterone thrown my way for one day," Carmen laughed shaking her head with amusement. "What'd our witness have to say?"

"Well, Natalie gave me a pretty good description of the guy," Adrian informed. "And, she said that the van had severe body damage along the right side."

"That narrows the search a little bit," Chris interjected, wiping the sweat from his brow.

"I also found it interesting that she said that as she was talking with the dispatcher, she overhead another dispatcher call for other units to assist you guys," Adrian continued. "At that precise moment, the suspect jumped into his van and began backing out of the driveway."

"So it's possible that this guy has a police scanner," Chris declared glancing at Carmen. "I guess we need to start using our tactical channel."

"Yeah, that's a good idea," Carmen agreed. "I also want to make sure that we have an officer over at Natalie's house for the next few days. We don't need to hand this guy another innocent person to kill."

"Did you all find anything inside the house?" Adrian inquired.

"Not one damn thing," Chris responded. "What would be so important to this fruitcake that he would risk coming back for?"

"You haven't talked to the coroner yet have you?" Adrian asked.

"No, we haven't," Carmen confirmed.

"Mike told me earlier today that he discovered an item that may be crucial in solving this case."

"Well, what is it?" Carmen asked, her eyes wide with childlike anticipation.

"Remember how much blood was in this last victim's hair?"

"Yeah, so what?" Chris shrugged.

"Mike found a gold bracelet all tangled up in it," Adrian explained excitedly. "He's already checked with the victim's relatives and it doesn't belong to the victim."

"Do you think it could be the suspect's?" Chris asked.

"Who else could it belong to?" Carmen countered slapping him lightly in the shoulder.

"All Mike would tell me is that it has someone's initials engraved on it," Adrian remarked.

"I'll head over to talk with Mike," Carmen declared. "Chris, why don't you take the car and see if the crime lab was able to get anything off those vases or if they found a match for that fingerprint yet. I'll have Adrian drop me off at the coroner's office and you can meet me there. Is that okay with everyone?"

"That's fine with me," Chris said climbing into the unmarked squad car. "I'll catch you all later."

"Yeah, it's fine with me too," Adrian chimed in heading over to her squad car with Carmen on her heels.

Chris backed out of the driveway as Adrian and Carmen climbed into Adrian's squad car. Carmen began to fill Adrian in on the details of the case since Captain Zebrowski had assigned Adrian to follow-up on the various leads called in by panic-stricken citizens. The number of calls that had flooded into dispatch was ridiculous. It seemed that everyone in Élan believed that either their oddball cousin, next door neighbor, or some other poor sap was the killer. Every call had to be investigated and cleared by Adrian.

As they pulled into the parking lot behind the coroner's office, Adrian put her hand on Carmen's shoulder. "You take care of yourself and if you need back up, just let me know," Adrian instructed.

"I will, I promise," Carmen replied.

"By the way," Adrian inquired, "I heard that you've been taking care of Zoë Childers."

Taken aback by the comment, Carmen tried sounding innocent, "Yes, I am."

"Will you tell her that I said hello?" Adrian requested. "And, that she better treat the new love in her life right."

Still surprised by the twist in conversation, Carmen looked out the car window as her cheeks became a soft shade of red. "I will," she stammered.

"It's written all over your face," Adrian stated matter-of-factly. "You are in love big time."

Carmen sat quietly for a moment dreading the answer to her next question. "How do you know Zoë?" she inquired unable to look Adrian in the eyes. "And, how well do you know her?"

"We went to college together," Adrian stated simply. "We've been friends ever since."

"Just friends?"

"Just friends," Adrian repeated as she cocked her head to one side and a slight grin appeared at the corners of her mouth.

"Oh, God," Carmen said. "What is it?"

"I know Zoë has had a thing for you for a long time," Adrian revealed.

"Really?" Carmen asked with a childish grin developing across her face.

Adrian smiled, "When you two first met it was because of a string of murders that started happening around the lower Westside. Zoë wasn't assigned to the case, but she took great interest in it because she knew one of the victims."

"She did?" Carmen asked dumbfounded.

Astonished, Adrian elaborated, "Her cousin was one of the victims. Didn't she tell you that?"

Carmen tried to speak, but her tongue wouldn't allow it. She finally managed to force out a one syllable word, "No."

"You informed Captain Zebrowski that you and Chris were quite capable of handling the case without any outside help," Adrian reminded.

"I did?" Carmen questioned dismayed.

"You did."

"I feel terrible," Carmen stated, thinking how hard that must have been for Zoë to swallow.

"Hey, don't forget that you caught that son of a bitch," Adrian interjected with admiration.

"I just wanted to make sure there weren't too many people on the case. There's more likely to be a screw-up that way," Carmen responded defensively.

"I know," Adrian declared. "Don't get your panties in a wad. All I was saying was that Zoë found you extremely sexy and intelligent. Since then, all she has wanted is to be with you, but you always seemed too busy."

"I wasn't too busy," Carmen stammered. "I just thought Zoë was unavailable."

"She sent you roses to thank you for catching that psychopath," Adrian stated. "You can't tell me that with that detective nose of yours, you weren't able to figure out who they were from."

"There wasn't a note," Carmen replied defending her position. Carmen would never admit to anyone that she had called the flower shop and used a little police persuasion to find out that Zoë was indeed the sender.

"Of course there wasn't a note," Adrian said dryly. "Do you think that straight-laced Detective Moore would like receiving flowers from another officer, especially a female one?"

"I guess not," Carmen sighed heavily, obviously hurt by the comment.

"Listen Carmen, I wasn't trying to slam you at all," Adrian offered. "We have all had a rough way to go and being a woman and a lesbian doesn't help. Zoë respected your position and how hard you had to fight to get there. She isn't at all the way she portrays herself at work. She is a very sensitive person and if you were wondering, she is very faithful."

"I believe that."

"I know you have heard all the rumors, but they're untrue," Adrian continued. "Zoë was brought up a lot like you. She has very strong morals and a heart of gold. The best advice I can give you is to never let her go."

"I won't," Carmen stated as her investigative skills picked up on the underlying happiness in Adrian's tone. "Are these words of wisdom stemming from somewhere or someone perhaps?"

"I'm just enjoying life."

"And, her name is?" Carmen encouraged sweetly.

"Rebecca," Adrian replied.

"Maybe we all could get together sometime," Carmen suggested.

"Sure, that would be great. I'll give you a call when you solve this case, if that's okay?"

Flattered by Adrian's faith in her, Carmen nodded her head, "That would be fine."

"Well, I'm here if you need help," Adrian offered. "Do what you do best, okay?"

"Okay."

With that, Carmen stepped from the squad car and headed up the walkway toward the shimmering glass doors of the coroner's office.

CHAPTER NINE

Carmen's footsteps echoed along the deserted corridor of the police station. She walked purposefully as she headed toward her division's office. In her briefcase, a gold bracelet with the initials J-P-B was secured in a clear evidence bag. Though she had called Chris earlier to see what he had learned, she didn't mention the bracelet. She had a feeling that if the killer was smart enough to have a police scanner, he was smart enough to use it to pick up cell phone conversations as well. Of course to do so, he would have to be in the vicinity and she'd bet money he was.

Chris had informed her that there were no prints on either vase collected from the two crime scenes. The latent print examiner, Daniel, had almost exhausted all outlets to find a match for the thumbprint recovered off the mirror. The crime lab offered nothing new on the DNA evidence that they had obtained. So, she and Chris had agreed to get a small task force together and meet at the station around 8 p.m.

As she approached, Carmen could hear a very heated discussion coming from behind the closed door of the detective's board room. She quietly entered the room and watched the interactions of her comrades. Chris, Adrian,

Officer Cooper, and Officer Allen were huddled around a large conference table challenging one another to prove that his or her theory was correct. The only one not participating was Zoë who seemed to be too engrossed in the paperwork she was reviewing to join in the 'I-have-more- testosterone-than-you' game.

Zoë's eyes traveled up from the page that she was studying and fixated on Carmen. Carmen struggled to keep from smiling as her heart seemed to do back flips into a pool of love only to resurface and do it all over again. Chris happened to catch a glimpse of Carmen out of the corner of his eye and he eased back into his chair. His sudden disengagement from the conversation alerted the rest of the group that they were no longer alone. They each sat back in their chairs as if Carmen had actually scolded them.

"Good evening, Carmen," Chris greeted motioning her over to the table. "We were just having a preliminary discussion about the case."

"I can see that," she replied striding across the room. "Hi, guys. How is everyone tonight?"

"Fine," Officer Allen responded.

"Speak for yourself," Adrian interjected cheerfully. "I'm starving."

"Yeah," Cooper chimed in, "Chris said you were bringing doughnuts."

"Is that so?" Carmen replied eyeing Chris wickedly as she set her briefcase down on the table.

"I didn't think you liked doughnuts," Zoë stated confused.

"I don't," Carmen confirmed. "But Chris thinks that everyone who is a cop needs at least one jelly-filled doughnut in their meal plan every day."

"Well, Popeye ate spinach every day," Chris argued.

"Oh, now those two food groups are comparable in nutritional value," Adrian teased sarcastically.

"And, Popeye was a sailor, not a cop," Officer Allen reminded. "You'd be more on track if you had used Wimpy in your analogy."

"Well," Chris said defeated, "I'll gladly pay you Tuesday for a doughnut today."

The group laughed. Carmen grabbed a metal gray folding chair and set it across the table from Zoë. She unlatched the clasps of the briefcase and removed the evidence bag that contained the bracelet and set it off to the side. She also took out a spiral bound notebook that contained her personal thoughts about the case before securing the clasps back into place and setting the briefcase onto the floor. She took her seat as Chris cleared his throat to get everyone's attention.

Chris stood up, straightened his tie, and ran his fingers through his thick black hair. "We've requested each of you to be here because as individuals you have proven yourself capable of handling a heavy caseload and getting results at the same time," he began. "This murder case is taking precedence over everything else right now. Carmen and I have determined that this case will not be solved by individual effort, but as a team. It is now 8:15 p.m. and this guy is still out there."

"So, what do we know so far?" Cooper pressed.

"Zoë?" Chris answered taking his seat. "Do you want to take it from here?"

"Sure," she stated glancing over at Carmen as she shuffled through some paperwork. "I decided to run a motor vehicle check for all persons owning a brown van in the last five years in our county. As you can imagine the list was long, but after talking with Chris and obtaining a better description of the suspect from our witness, I ran another check. There are approximately 22 white males who have brown vans registered in this county."

"So, we have to check out 22 people? Are you crazy?" Officer Allen interjected skeptically. "What if he isn't any of them?"

Zoë's eyes furrowed with anger, "If you will let me finish, instead of interrupting, I was getting to that."

Officer Allen was taken off guard by Zoë's reaction and offered his apology, "Sorry, Detective Childers, I just want to get this guy off our streets."

"So do I," Zoë reiterated. "We ran background checks and most of the suspects were eliminated for one reason or another. We have 11 possibilities left. Six of them have a criminal record, but that doesn't mean anything. Three of them registered a brown van within the last year. What they do all have in common is that they are white males and have brown hair."

"Damn, that's still quite a few people to check out." Officer Cooper stated disappointedly.

"Well, it doesn't mean any one of them is the right guy, but it is a start," Zoë sighed, visibly irritated by the lack of optimism.

"Zoë, do you have the list here with the owners' names on it?" Carmen inquired.

"Of course, Carmen," Zoë said sweetly.

"Can I see the list?" Carmen questioned, blushing slightly.

Zoë handed Carmen the list and touched her hand ever so slightly just to feel the warmth of her skin. Carmen accepted the list and was thankful for her long sleeve shirt that concealed the goose bumps that Zoë had invoked. Carmen pulled out her notes and began scanning the list. The group was silent as her index finger traveled down the length of the list before stopping on one name.

The tension had mounted to an excruciating limit and Cooper finally couldn't stand waiting anymore. "Come on Carmen," he insisted. "What the hell is going on?"

Carmen pushed away from the table and stood up. She couldn't resist smiling. "Earlier today, I went to the coroner's office and recovered a piece of evidence that was entangled in the last victim's hair," she announced triumphantly holding up the baggie containing the bracelet. "There are three initials engraved and some sort of insignia on the bracelet."

"Do the initials match one of the names on the list?" Chris inquired.

"Take a look for yourself," Carmen instructed handing Chris the evidence bag and the list of names.

Chris peered through the evidence bag and ran down the list of names. Satisfied, he handed the list and bracelet to Zoë. One by one, each member of the task force reviewed the evidence with Cooper being the last one to see it. He tapped his left index finger lightly against his lips and suddenly grinned. "Carmen, I know that insignia!" he exclaimed. "My wife graduated from that college."

"Don't keep us in suspense," Carmen declared.

"It's the Indiana University's insignia," Cooper announced proudly.

"Okay, we need to settle down," Carmen reminded hushing the conversations that had spurred up in light of this new found lead. "Cooper, I want you and Allen to find out this guy's address, where he works, and anything else."

"We're on it," Cooper said grabbing the list with the suspect's name after Zoë had circled it in bright red ink.

Cooper and Allen bolted toward the door like kids going outside for recess. They almost plowed down one of the evening dispatchers as she unexpectedly entered the room.

"Sorry!" Cooper said over his shoulder as he chased Allen through the doorway and down the hallway.

"What brings you down here tonight?" Carmen asked as the dispatcher hurried over to her.

"He struck again," the dispatcher gasped almost incoherently.

"What?" Zoë demanded getting to her feet.

"He struck again!" the dispatcher repeated. "Captain Zebrowski is requesting all of you to the crime scene immediately."

The group was momentarily paralyzed. Time seemed to have warped around them and they were unable to make their minds generate any action. Carmen felt the strength in her legs vacate her muscles leaving her wondering if she would fall over if she made any sudden movements. Her arms were also subjected to this humbling feeling. All the noise crackling from the radio clipped to the dispatcher's belt ceased to exist as her jumbled up thoughts screamed at her. Then, the moment passed and the adrenaline started pumping. "What's the address?" Carmen demanded.

The dispatcher handed Carmen a slip of paper. Carmen read the address and her hands began to tremble. She raised her eyes to meet Chris'. Chris saw the apprehensiveness and grabbed the slip of paper out of her hands. He peered down at the note and the color in his face drained within mere seconds. "Phone! I need a phone!" he cried out, running toward his desk.

Frantically, Chris snatched up the receiver and pounded the small numeric keypad. Zoë and Adrian exchanged worried glances and looked to Carmen for an explanation of his erratic behavior. Carmen felt her heart sinking and tears springing to her eyes as she listened to her partner plead for his wife to pick up the phone. She didn't take her attention off him as she informed Zoë and Adrian about the note. "The address is on 28th street," she said softly.

"What does that have to do with Chris?" Adrian urged.

"Chris and his wife live at 601 28th street," Carmen answered consciously aware that Cuffs was presently staying there too.

"There was confusion in the two 911 calls we received," the dispatcher explained.

"There were two calls?" Carmen questioned as she overheard Chris talking to his wife.

"Yeah, the first caller said that there had been a murder at the Duhn residence on 28th street," the dispatcher replied.

"And the second call?" Zoë interrupted impatiently.

"It came in about three minutes later," the dispatcher informed. "The woman was hysterical. She kept repeating to send help to 106 28th street because someone had murdered her neighbor."

Carmen heard Chris tell his wife that he loved her over and over again. She refocused her attention back on the dispatcher, "Was the first call from a man?"

"Yes, why?" the dispatcher asked, realizing the answer almost immediately. "You don't think it was the killer, do you?"

"Yes," Carmen snapped unintentionally. "Did you put the audiotape in evidence?"

"Yes, ma'am," the dispatcher answered slightly defensive.

"Good work," Carmen replied.

"Thank you," the dispatcher said relieved. "No one else wanted to be the one that relayed the news to Detective Duhn."

"It's a hard position to be in," Carmen stated.

"Can I do anything?" the dispatcher questioned compassionately.

"Give me a minute," Carmen replied. She turned around and walked over to Chris' desk. She watched helplessly as Chris covered his face with his hands. "Are you okay?" she asked softly.

"Yeah," Chris muttered. "She was in the shower and didn't hear the phone ringing right away."

"That's understandable," Carmen offered objectively already knowing his follow-up question.

"You don't think he was going after my wife, do you?" he demanded. "It's just a coincidence, right?"

"Right," she agreed unable to look him in the eyes.

Chris stared at her unblinkingly. She could feel his eyes penetrating deep into her soul. Did the killer believe he had murdered Chris's wife or was he merely toying with them? She owed Chris more than a speculative response or a guarded answer. She owed him the truth, but would it cause more harm than good if she told him what the male caller had said?

"What are you not telling me?" Chris demanded, his voice shaking uncontrollably.

Carmen chose her words carefully. "Chris, the first call for help was from a male caller," she informed evenly. "Um, he said there had been a murder."

"So, they automatically assumed it was my wife?" he yelled slamming his fist against the desk.

"The caller specified your residence by name," Carmen said bracing for the impact of her words.

Chris's anger was apparent, but fear for his wife was now driving his emotions. "We need to go, right now!" he choked. "Tell Captain Zebrowski I'll be there as soon as I stop by my house and check on Mary."

"I'm going with him," Adrian stated, racing after Chris. "We'll meet you there."

Carmen spun around to face the dispatcher. "Look, no one comes in this room," she instructed. "Lock the door and call one of the security officers to guard it."

"I'll take care of it," the dispatcher replied.

"No one comes in," Carmen reiterated. "All the evidence is in here."

"I understand," the dispatcher assured.

Zoë grabbed Carmen's arm and dragged her out of the board room. They ran down the stairs skipping multiple steps at a time. The pounding of their footsteps roared through the corridor. Stride for stride they ran without stopping until they were at the security desk. Carmen stopped one of the officers who had just dropped off his nightly reports and demanded his keys. Without hesitation, he handed them to her. "I'll be at the crime scene on 28th street!" she hollered.

The officer overheard Carmen yell "thank you" over her shoulder. He smiled at the security guard sitting behind the desk, "Is there anyone who can give me a ride home?"

• • •

Zoë and Carmen climbed into the squad car. Carmen's mind raced back to the conversation she had with her boss, Captain Zebrowski, earlier that day. He had paged her while she was at the coroner's office. When she called him back, he had informed her that he had pulled the officers watching over their homes back to street patrol. He believed that they were wasting their time and that Chris had made too big of deal about the situation. She pushed the accelerator to the floorboard in anger and squealed the tires as she exited the parking lot.

Zoë turned on the emergency lights feeling the familiar rush of adrenaline kicking in. "I forgot what an awesome feeling it is to be racing to a scene," she shouted in order for Carmen to hear her over the siren.

"Me too," Carmen hollered back. "We're usually the cleanup crew, you know?"

"I know," Zoë agreed noticing the tension on Carmen's face. "Promise me something?"

"What is it?"

Zoë leaned over and kissed Carmen tenderly on the cheek, "Don't go after this guy alone."

"Okay," Carmen replied glancing over at her. "I hadn't planned on it."

"I don't want you to get hurt," Zoë elaborated. "And, you're stubborn enough to go after him because he has targeted your partner."

"I'm not that stubborn," Carmen argued.

"Yes, you are."

"So, what if I am?" Carmen questioned turning onto 28th Street. "This lunatic is making it personal."

"That's true," Zoë agreed. "Just let me be by your side when you catch him, okay?"

Carmen gave her a reassuring smile, "You mean when we catch him, right?"

"Yeah, when we catch him," Zoë repeated. "I promise."

Carmen released the death grip she had on the steering wheel and gave Zoë's thigh a gentle squeeze. Her rage for her captain slowly dissipated and she concentrated on maneuvering past the two squad cars that had part of 28th street blocked. She glanced over at the passenger seat and was briefly distracted by Zoë's beautiful profile. She knew without a doubt that between her intuitive investigative skills and Zoë's knowledge on serial killers, they made an unbeatable team at work. She also knew that they made an incredible team outside of work as well.

CHAPTER TEN

Chris whipped into his driveway and came to a screeching halt in front of his ranch style home. Down the road, he could see the multitude of red and blue lights corrupting the night sky. Adrian waited as he threw open the driver's side door and sprinted up the walkway to where his wife was waiting with Cuffs underneath a yellow tinted porch light. He took her in his arms and kissed her long and passionately being careful not to squish Cuffs.

Adrian noticed that Mary was dressed in jeans and a baggy sweatshirt. She couldn't help but wonder what Chris might be up to. She watched as he locked their front door and escorted Mary toward the squad car. "This isn't a good idea, my friend," she thought staring down at her hands.

Mary climbed into the back seat with Cuffs still nestled in her arms. Chris situated himself once again behind the steering wheel. He checked the rearview mirror and eased the unmarked squad car back down the driveway. "I told her on the phone that she needed to be dressed," he said, avoiding looking at Adrian directly. "I don't want her to be here alone."

Adrian knew that having an unauthorized family member at a crime scene was against the rules, but this wasn't the time for a standard operating procedure lecture. Mary wouldn't be safe until the killer was caught. If the killer figured out he'd made a mistake, he would more than likely come back to finish the job. She knew that Chris realized this as well although he didn't dare tell his wife. "It's probably better that she does come with us," Adrian agreed flawlessly. "Besides, while you're off investigating, I'll need someone to keep me company."

"Thank you," Chris said appreciatively, knowing that Adrian was going out on a limb with him. But, he also knew without a doubt that she would sacrifice her badge if it meant saving a life. The qualities that Adrian had always portrayed were truly what made a cop a great one. A cop needed to be sincere, honest, and brave, but, most of all, compassionate. Compassion would keep Adrian by Mary's side because it was the right thing to do no matter what it cost.

Chris stomped on the accelerator causing the car to wrench forward. Within seconds, he pulled up next to Carmen and Zoë who had also just arrived. Carmen quickly got out of the squad car and rushed over to open the door for Mary. She was relieved to see Cuffs safe and sound in her lap. As soon as Mary stepped out of the car, Cuffs jumped into her arms.

"How's my good boy?" Carmen asked in a voice usually reserved for a baby. Cuffs licked the tip of her nose and his tail wagged feverishly. Carmen averted her attention away from Cuffs momentarily and her voice grew serious, "You okay, Mary?"

"She doesn't know a lot right now," Chris growled. "So, just keep your mouth shut."

"Well, I think she should know," Carmen answered vehemently, outraged by Chris' lack of professionalism.

"I'll fill her in while you all are investigating the crime scene," Adrian pleaded, trying to keep Chris and

Carmen from ending up on the 11 o'clock news. She could just picture a news team broadcasting Chris sprawled out on the ground after Carmen slugged him for acting like such a jerk. "I'll tell her only what is pertinent at the moment, okay?" Adrian added in response to the look of anguish on Chris' face.

"Okay," he agreed reluctantly. He embraced his wife one more time and managed to muster up a smile, "I love you, baby."

"I love you too, honey," Mary replied softly. "Now, go do your job. I'll be fine."

Chris released his embrace slowly and Mary accepted Cuffs back into her arms. Cuffs nestled his body against her baggy sweatshirt and closed his eyes. Chris watched helplessly as Adrian guided Mary away from the crime scene and across the street to the less conspicuous place of a neighbor's front yard. He turned toward Carmen, "I'm sorry for snapping at you."

"It's okay," Carmen said thinking of Zoë. "I would be the same way if someone I loved was caught in this predicament."

• • •

Carmen gave her name to the officer posted just outside the front door of the crime scene. She turned to see if Chris had followed, but he was still standing at the base of steps leading up to the porch completely paralyzed. Sympathizing with his agony, she walked back down the steps and pulled him aside. "Why don't you talk to the officer who was first on scene," Carmen stated knowing full well Chris was wrestling with the idea that this could have been his house.

"Okay," he answered despondently.

"See if you can find anything out from the neighbor who found her as well," Carmen encouraged.

"Alright," he stammered. "That's a good way to divide our efforts."

He pivoted on his heels and headed over toward Officer Leigh who happened to be the first officer on the scene. Carmen's heart went out to Chris as he fought to keep his personal feelings under control. She waived Zoë over and waited for her outside the front door. Zoë checked in with the officer and followed Carmen into the house. They proceeded toward the kitchen where Mike was waiting for them.

It was essential to the integrity of the investigation to preserve as much of the crime scene as possible. No one else had been allowed to come into the residence except for two paramedics and the coroner. They had been logged in at the door and checked off as they exited. At the time, Mike was the only one left in the kitchen.

Carmen stepped around the corner into the kitchen. She thought that she had prepared herself for the horrific scene she was about to witness, but she had to force herself to keep from throwing up. Never before had she seen such a complete disregard for human life. The poor lifeless naked body of a woman in her thirties was sitting on the kitchen table. A cold steel chain was wrapped around her neck and strung up to a hook on the ceiling keeping her body from slumping over. The kitchen light that had been hanging from the hook was resting on top of the stove. She had obviously been positioned like that post-evisceration because her hair was matted with dried blood in a tangled mess.

Carmen carefully moved over to the body and examined the victim's right hand that had been taped to her chest with the middle finger extended. The killer had eviscerated her like the others, but this time instead of a handwritten note, he had left a message in blood across the back wall.

"YOU ALMOST CAUGHT ME, BUT I GOT THIS ONE. YOU'RE ALWAYS ONE STEP BEHIND ME AND FOR NOW I'M DONE."

"Jesus, this guy is really messed up." Zoë said disgusted.

"I think the middle finger being taped up was an especially nice touch, don't you, Carmen?" Mike asked sarcastically. "Any thoughts on why he did that?"

"It's simple," Carmen answered. "He thinks he's won."

"I'd agree with that," Zoë interjected.

"By the way," Mike said, "I've almost finished my report on the second victim."

"Anything of interest?" Carmen prodded, flipping open her notepad.

"Same cause of death as the first victim," Mike reported. "Strangled and eviscerated in that order."

"No carvings in the pelvic region?" Zoë questioned.

"On the contrary," Mike replied, "but I'm still working on it."

"Another word?" Carmen inquired.

"I think so, but I'm trying to figure out what the heck the killer was trying to spell."

"What do you mean?" Carmen quizzed, sketching the new crime scene in pencil.

"I've been able to establish that two of the letters are 'D' and 'N'," he said slipping on a fresh pair of latex gloves. "But, I'm having a hard time deciphering the letter that was carved in between. It could be a 'Q', 'O', or 'U'. I just need more time."

"Time is the one thing we don't have," Carmen said, examining the victim's wrists.

"Then, let's get started," Zoë interjected.

Carmen and Zoë began examining the area surrounding the victim. Debra had arrived with the rest of the crime scene unit and taken the liberty to begin snapping evidence photos. She was careful not to get in Carmen and Zoë's way. She photographed the position of the kitchen light before Zoë dusted it for prints. Once finished, another crime lab technician slipped it into a large evidence bag. Anything of interest was photographed first, dusted, collected, and labeled for identification purposes.

For the next three hours, Carmen and Zoë took more pictures, collected blood samples, bagged hair follicles, dusted for fingerprints, and theorized. Zoë found a shoe print left in some blood underneath the kitchen table. Carmen located the fresh vase of flowers in the living room and the towel that the killer used to clean himself up with shoved in the bottom of a trashcan in the garage.

When they finally emerged from the crime scene and stepped out onto the porch, it was close to 1:20 a.m. There were very few people still at the scene. All the news crews had left and most of the neighbors had gone on home. The crime lab was loading up the last of their equipment into their van. There were two patrol cars stationed along the curb unintentionally blocking in Chris, Mary, and Adrian who were conversing inside the borrowed police cruiser.

When Chris noticed Carmen and Zoë on the porch, he opened the driver's side door and hurried over to them. "I talked with Cooper and Allen earlier," he declared, waving to one of the officers sitting on the hood of his squad car that now would be a good time to move. "I told them that we should all meet up at the police station tomorrow morning around 9:30 a.m. Is that okay with the two of you?"

"That's fine with me," Zoë responded.

"We need to discuss the message left behind by the killer," Carmen began.

"Not tonight," Chris begged. "I don't want to talk about that tonight, okay?"

Carmen knew that he was putting on a tough act for his wife's sake and that in reality he was scared and angry. "Alright, not tonight," she promised. "Are you two going home tonight?"

"Nah, we decided to stay at a hotel nearby." Chris raised his eyebrows rapidly up and down and gave her a guileful grin. "Besides, I need to spend some one-on-one time with my wife, if you know what I mean?"

"Yeah, I get the message," Carmen replied. "But tomorrow we need to get back to work, okay?"

Chris rolled his eyes, "You sound like my mother." With that, he ran back to the squad car and started the engine.

Adrian climbed out of the back seat with Cuffs in her arms. She closed the passenger door and waived good-bye to Chris and Mary. She strutted over to where Carmen and Zoë were standing scratching Cuff's belly all the way. "Can you drop me off at the police station?" she asked. "I need to pick up my car."

"Sure, Adrian," Zoë said, eyeing Carmen mischievously. "We don't have a problem with that, do we, babe?"

"Whatever my woman says," Carmen replied.

"You two are making me sick!" Adrian cried. "Please tell me that the two of you can control yourselves until I get out of the car."

"I can't promise a thing," Zoë responded, scanning the length of Carmen's body with her eyes.

"Me either," Carmen smiled.

"There is something seriously wrong with the two of you," Adrian interjected. "I mean you would think this murder would take the sex drive right out of you."

Carmen was slightly offended even though she knew Adrian was kidding around. She took a couple of seconds to think about her response. Still, the crispness in her voice was evident and it sent a message loud and clear. "This is how I deal with times like this," Carmen defended. "It doesn't mean that I'm not completely obsessed with catching this guy."

"I know," Adrian replied apologetically. "I was just giving you a hard time."

Zoë rubbed her hand comfortingly between Carmen's shoulder blades. "Easy, baby," she soothed. "We all have different ways of handling things. Sometimes the best way for one person to handle a situation is not the same for another."

All three of them stood in silence. The loss of human life was hard, but when dealing with such a horrific demoralization of life it was worse, even for the most seasoned officers. Carmen understood that people sometimes forgot that, although an officer is sworn to protect and serve regardless of the situation at hand, they are still human. And, as a human being, it could be quite exhausting concealing emotions until one was off duty. Sometimes, even then, there was no outlet.

"I know we're going to catch this little bastard!" Carmen declared.

"No doubt," Adrian replied, playfully punching Carmen in the arm.

"Well then, we better get going, so I can get some rest," Zoë said earnestly. "I feel like I've run an entire marathon and my shoulder is killing me."

The three of them climbed into the squad car with Carmen at the wheel. No one spoke on the way to the station. They all knew what to expect. Tomorrow would be a long and tedious day. The killer had indicated that he would stop killing for the moment. In turn, that could be interpreted to mean a variety of things. He might be thinking of laying low for awhile, starting up in a different city, or ending his killing spree all together.

Statistically, though, Carmen and Zoë knew that the majority of serial killers wanted to be caught for the sheer thrill of notoriety. However, there had been a few, such as the Zodiac and Green River killers, whose murdering sprees ended abruptly and were never heard from again. Carmen knew she would do everything in her power to not let this serial killer vanish into thin air and become another infamous celebrity thanks to some sap writing a book about it.

• • •

Carmen let Cuffs explore the small yard right in front of Zoë's condo. He was determined to mark every blade of grass so that all other dogs in the neighborhood knew that this was now his territory. Zoë waited for them on the front porch with her hand on her gun constantly scanning the street for a killer that might be using the cover of darkness to sneak up on them. When Cuffs was finished, he followed Carmen inside and made himself at home on the couch. Zoë locked the front door and waited for Carmen to fill a small bowl with water for Cuffs.

"Here you go, buddy," Carmen said, setting the bowl down on the kitchen floor. "I'll pick you up some dog food tomorrow."

Cuffs' ears perked up, but he didn't budge from the couch. "I think he's worn out," Zoë said, stepping over to Carmen. "And, so is his mom."

"I'm a little tired," Carmen admitted.

"Well, let's get to bed," Zoë encouraged. "If we fall asleep in the next ten minutes, we might actually get four hours of shut-eye."

"Do you want me to sleep on the couch?" Carmen asked not wanting to be presumptuous.

"Of course not," Zoë chuckled. "Get your cute butt in the bedroom."

"Yes, ma'am," Carmen replied hurrying past Zoë.

"Hey, wait for me," Zoë said chasing after her. "I need some intense, personal attention, you know?"

"Is that so?" Carmen inquired pulling her shirt off over her head and tossing it onto the floor. "What kind of attention do you have in mind?"

Zoë put her hand on the light switch as Carmen unzipped her jeans and allowed them to fall to the floor. "Get into bed," she coaxed. "I'll show you what kind of attention I have in mind."

• • •

Carmen and Zoë arrived at the police station just before 7 a.m. They immediately began comparing notes and discovered that each victim had a set routine that they rarely veered from. They were single women with no children and no family members living with them. They traveled the same route to and from work each day. They were possibly befriended by the killer due to the absence of forced entry into their homes. There were no physical similarities that might narrow the scope of what type of women the killer went after. And the three victims did not know one another, nor did they have any mutual friends.

"So, what else do we have to work with?" Zoë prompted aloud, racking her brain to make some sense out of the seemingly random acts of violence.

"All three victims had their windpipes crushed from strangulation before being eviscerated," Carmen replied reading over the autopsy reports that Mike had left on her desk before they had arrived. "Furthermore, each of them had a word cut into their skin just above the pelvic bone."

"Have you figured out what they mean yet?" Zoë inquired.

"I feel like it's on the tip of my tongue," Carmen said exasperated. "Victim #1 had the word 'more' slashed into the pelvic region by the same knife that was used for her evisceration. The second victim had the word 'done' misspelled and carved into her with a very different cutting instrument, like a scalpel. That's why Mike had such a hard time with it. "

"How did the killer spell it?" Zoë inquired.

"D-U-N," Carmen stated.

"But the killer didn't leave that cutting instrument behind," Zoë reminded. "So, that makes me think that maybe he started wondering if he was being too overzealous or accidentally cut himself and some of his blood transferred onto it."

"You might be right," Carmen said, flipping to the next page of the autopsy report.

"What about victim #3?" Zoë pressed.

"Victim #3 had the word 'coper' cut into her," Carmen revealed. "Mike believes the killer used the same weapon to carve the word he did on the second victim."

"So, why didn't he just keeping using the knives he obtained from the victim's homes?" Zoë wondered aloud.

"Maybe he needed a better writing utensil," Carmen suggested.

Zoë remained silent as she processed the reasoning behind the change in weapon. Carmen glanced at her wristwatch and noticed it was five minutes until nine o'clock in the morning. She closed her eyes and allowed her head to fall forward gently stretching the muscles in her neck. "There has to be some sort of connection between the inscriptions," she stated.

"Well, the only word that has been spelled correctly is 'more'," Zoë recalled. "And, what significance do these words even have?"

Carmen could sense the intensity of Zoë's stare. She opened her eyes to meet Zoë's gaze and inhaled the sweet scent of her perfume. She leaned forward and grasped Zoë's long slender fingers. She stroked them delicately with her thumb and reached up with her other hand to gently touch Zoë's face. "God, you're beautiful," Carmen said softly.

"Thank you," Zoë whispered as she closed her eyes and enjoyed the attention that Carmen was lavishing on her. "So baby, what do you think?"

Carmen could barely pull her eyes from Zoë's lovely face, "I think he was trying to tell us something in his last message."

"You mean the part about how he is always one step ahead of us," Zoë questioned opening her eyes.

"Yeah," Carmen confirmed. "Don't you think it's a little odd that he didn't misspell any of his messages?"

"He probably had them written out before hand," Zoë stated matter-of-factly. "I mean, spell check is a wonderful thing, you know."

"I know," Carmen agreed. "He just seems too meticulous to misspell such simple words."

"Can I see the autopsy reports?"

"Sure," Carmen said, pushing them over to her. "If we look at it like jigsaw puzzle and spell the words correctly, we'd have 'more', 'done', and 'copper'.

"That doesn't make any sense either," Zoë declared as she scanned the reports.

"We're missing something," Carmen said slightly irritated.

Zoë gently raised Carmen's hand to her sensuous lips and kissed the top of her hand. "Baby, I have no idea what those words could refer to," she replied shuffling the reports back into numerical order. "Maybe when Chris gets here, he'll have some idea."

Carmen's eyes lit up, "Zoë, that's it."

"What's it?"

Carmen rustled through her briefcase and pulled out a newspaper clipping. Excitedly, she sprang from her seat, went around the table, and knelt down beside Zoë. She held the newspaper article up to where Zoë could see it. "Last night a woman was found murdered in an apartment complex off of Oceanview Parkway," Carmen read aloud. "Blah, blah, blah. Investigating this brutal attack are Élan's finest, Detectives Christopher Duhn and Carmen Moore."

Zoë grabbed the newspaper and scanned the rest of the article; "Holy shit!" she cried out, her eyes wide open with astonishment. "It also mentions that Officer Bryce Cooper was one of the first on the scene and quotes him saying that the cause of death was currently undetermined."

An eerie quiet developed between them as they thought about the possibility of the killer personalizing the victims with the names of the police personnel investigating the case. Finally, Zoë broke the silence and tried to hide the uneasiness of her tone. "There are a few things though that don't make any sense," she said softly.

"Like the missing letters?" Carmen inquired.

"There has to be some significance in the third letter missing in each name," Zoë proposed.

Carmen's eyes were glassy and unfocused. Her face was almost a ghostly white. Zoë slid her arms around Carmen's waist protectively and gently nuzzled her head against Carmen's breasts that were hidden by her blue satiny dress shirt and blue pinstriped black dress coat. Carmen returned this advance by encircling her arms gingerly around Zoë's shoulders and planting a kiss on her forehead.

"Are you okay?" Zoë asked easing back into the chair just in case someone unexpectedly bolted into the room.

"I'll be fine," Carmen replied engulfed in guilt. She couldn't help but feel that if she had done something differently or been more observant that first night, she might have stopped the death of another poor innocent woman. She knew that there really was no way of knowing, but she still felt responsible.

Furthermore, Carmen had convinced herself that the killer had no way of knowing that it was her coming home from walking Cuffs. Now, in lieu of this new discovery, it was quite possible that he did know and had planned to kill her if he needed to. Tears were threatening to spill over and cascade down her cheeks as Carmen looked up at Zoë. Her jaw was clenched shut trying to still the quivering of her bottom lip. The helplessness in Carmen's voice was evident; "He would have killed me."

"Baby, we're going to get him," Zoë stated. "Besides," she reminded, "you're still here."

"I know," Carmen choked, "but I should have sensed something was wrong that night."

"This isn't your fault," Zoë declared. "Stop beating yourself up over it."

"I can't help it," Carmen replied.

"He would have tried to kill you had you interrupted him."

"I know," Carmen whispered.

"He tried to kill you the other night," Zoë reminded, squeezing Carmen's hand. "And, he'll try again."

"I just don't understand why," Carmen said. "I need to know why."

"Carmen, let's say he didn't choose his first victim at random," Zoë suggested, dreading the effect that her next statement might have. "It's quite possible he chose you."

"Me?" Carmen responded shifting uncomfortably in her seat.

"Honey," Zoë attempted. "I'm sorry, but you know that theory makes the most sense."

"I know," Carmen replied half-heartedly, staring at an invisible spot on the carpet.

"Look at me," Zoë pleaded. "Even if he did choose you, it still isn't your fault."

"But why does it feel that way?" Carmen questioned.

"Because you care," Zoë said softly.

Carmen cupped Zoë's face in the palms of her hands and stared deep into her eyes. "I trust your opinion," Carmen stated truthfully. "It just took me a minute to accept."

"I'm sorry, baby," Zoë responded, her heart aching to come clean about how deeply she cared for Carmen. "It's my professional opinion and my personal one, too."

"I know," Carmen said with a new sense of determination. "Let's see if we can figure out where the rest of puzzle pieces fit."

CHAPTER ELEVEN

At 9:30 a.m., Chris arrived with a doughnut box under his arm. Zoë quietly chuckled as Carmen transformed back into the 'hard as nails' detective that everyone believed she was. When Carmen said hello to Chris, her voice was as smooth as silk, her shoulders were squared, her back erect, and her confidence evident in her walk.

"How are you?" Carmen whispered sensing a quiet rage brewing underneath Chris's calm exterior as she hugged him.

"I've had better days," Chris answered simply. "Let's get to work."

The three of them sat down around the oak conference table and Chris and Zoë dove into the doughnut box. "We've made some progress with how this guy is selecting his victims," Carmen stated walking over to the row of cabinets that lined the back wall.

"And?" Chris mumbled, biting into his chocolate cream-filled doughnut.

"He selected us, Chris," Carmen stated bluntly, removing a couple of napkins from one of the cabinet drawers.

"What do you mean he selected us?" Chris demanded, washing down another bite with a sip of coffee.

"She means," Zoë interjected, "he selected victims based on their proximity to his intended targets."

"Are you telling me that this lunatic killed those women based on where we live?" Chris asked astonished.

"Yes," Carmen answered just before the clock on the back wall announced it was ten o'clock in the morning with a series of chimes.

"This case just gets stranger by the minute," Chris said, graciously accepting the napkin that Carmen handed him.

• • •

Adrian, Cooper and Allen rushed into the room and joined them around the table. "Sorry," Adrian offered. "Captain Zebrowski had us in his office for an apparent quick meeting that lasted forty-five minutes.

"We completely understand," Carmen assured, taking her seat. "You wouldn't believe how many meetings Chris and I have been late to for that exact reason."

"Did we miss anything?" Cooper asked, eyeing the doughnut box.

"Sorry Cooper," Chris chuckled, "it's empty."

"Always a day late and a dollar short," Cooper replied with a grin.

"It sure seems that way," Allen said, fighting back a yawn.

Carmen noticed that everyone looked totally exhausted and each was downing their doses of caffeine. Chris, of course, had a never-ending rotation of caffeine with the large steaming cup of coffee in one hand and the last chocolate donut in the other. Both Cooper and Allen were guzzling twenty ounce bottles of Mountain Dew for their morning feast. Adrian seemed to be the only one with enough sense to eat something for breakfast. She munched quietly on a cream cheese covered bagel and chased it with a French Vanilla espresso.

Carmen handed each of them a packet of information that she and Zoë had put together just before Chris had arrived. Each packet included a list of all the evidence recovered from the crime scenes, copies of her sketches, the autopsy reports, and a synopsis of the facts that had been gathered so far. "I want each of you to review the information enclosed and make sure we haven't overlooked anything up to this point," she instructed. "Then, we'll have Cooper and Allen enlighten us on their findings."

Everyone began reviewing their individual packets and Carmen watched their reactions closely. The fact that the killer had personalized the victims' bodies with hers, Chris', and Cooper's names would only add to the escalating hatred for this individual. She needed to ensure that the members of the task force were capable of putting their emotions aside. She had already made the decision that she wasn't going to allow her personal feelings to interfere with the investigation. She would follow protocol and so would her team or she would be forced to remove them from it.

"Does anyone have any questions before we get started?" Chris inquired when he had everyone's attention.

"How did we miss what the words carved in the victim's meant?" Adrian questioned baffled.

"We just did," Carmen stated matter-of-factly.

"They say hindsight is 20/20," Zoë interjected.

"Has there ever been a serial killer that's chosen victim's based on the proximity of cops before?" Allen inquired.

"I don't think so," Zoë stated thoughtfully. "But, you can guarantee that I'll be researching it as soon as we solve this case."

"Well, there's a first time for everything," Chris reminded.

"What I don't understand is if the killer was choosing victim's based on the proximity of your homes," Allen challenged, "why did he choose the second victim?"

"Now that was the residence off of Rampart Road, right?" Zoë asked flipping through her notes. "The one where Natalie lives across the street, correct?"

"Yes," Carmen answered.

"Who's Natalie?" Allen asked scanning his notes.

"Our witness," Carmen replied. "She was the one who alerted us when the suspect returned to the crime scene."

"And, who will hopefully grow up and become a detective," Chris added. "She's extremely observant."

"Yeah, she has a good head on her shoulders," Adrian chimed in.

"Back to Allen's question," Carmen interrupted. "I think Cooper can answer this better than anyone else."

"You can?" Allen pressed turning to Cooper.

"I used to live down the road," Cooper said with a shrug. "I moved about eight months ago."

"So, it's feasible to believe that our suspect started planning these murders prior to Cooper moving," Allen speculated.

"It's possible," Zoë confirmed.

"What about the fingerprint that Carmen discovered?" Adrian questioned. "I don't see that listed in the evidence section."

"It's been eliminated," Chris replied.

"Why?" Adrian questioned.

"The latent print examiner, Daniel, located the owner of the suspect fingerprint," Carmen elaborated. "It belonged to an illegal immigrant who helped Ms. Lopez with the occasional handyman tasks around her home."

"How did Daniel figure that out?" Cooper pondered aloud.

"The guy showed up for work yesterday afternoon," Carmen explained. "Sgt. Hammond was the one guarding the crime scene and translated what had happened with Ms. Lopez to him in Spanish."

"How did he take it?" Adrian asked compassionately.

"Not well," Carmen replied. "But, he did come down to the police station and get fingerprinted."

"We're not going to deport him, are we?" Cooper questioned, visibly disturbed by the possibility.

"We're not the Immigration and Naturalization Service," Carmen replied simply.

Cooper smiled, "No, we're not."

"Well, on that note," Carmen declared, "let's hear what you and Cooper discovered."

"Go ahead," Allen encouraged, nudging Cooper in the side.

"Alright," Cooper replied. "Allen and I found out some interesting things about our suspect last night including his current address."

"That's terrific," Chris said, successfully tossing his Styrofoam coffee cup into a trashcan about three feet away.

Cooper opened up his briefcase and removed a copy of their fact-finding report. He slid it over to Carmen and took a quick sip of his soda hoping to cure his dry mouth. He usually didn't feel so nervous when talking to a group, but this was different. He had spent all night contacting different police agencies and obtaining unsolved case reports. Allen, on the other hand, spent most of the night talking to the suspect's father. Cooper knew that what he was about to share with the group would ignite a chain of events that would hopefully help catch the killer. He prayed the information would at the very least be enough to obtain a search warrant for the suspect's residence.

Carmen scanned the fact-finding report and when she was finished she addressed the group candidly. "What Cooper is about to share with us is vital to solving this case," she began. "I want you to formulate an opinion based on the facts that you already know and what you will learn from Cooper's and Allen's impressive research. If anything he says spurs a question in your mind either write it down or ask it."

Everyone nodded their head in agreement. Carmen sat back down giving Cooper the floor. Cooper cleared his throat and took one last sip of his soda. "This is the background information for our suspect, Mr. John Patrick Burns," he began, his voice resonating with strength and pride. "John was born in Greenville, a small town in the state of Indiana. His father, who at that time was a Greenville road deputy, took on the responsibilities of being a single father when John's mother passed away in a house fire. The autopsy of his mother revealed that she did not die from smoke inhalation as previously thought, but from being strangled. At the time of the fire, John was five years old."

"That's a little creepy," Adrian commented under her breath jotting a few things down on her notepad.

"According to John's father, James, when John turned twenty-one he applied to become a road deputy," Cooper continued. "He was turned down because during the psychological evaluation of the hiring process, the psychologist reported that John had frequent anxiety attacks and a volatile temper."

"Now, we're getting somewhere," Zoë declared.

"What do you mean?" Adrian pressed licking the last of the cream cheese from the bagel off her fingers.

"Well, it's our first solid reference to his psychological stability," Zoë explained.

"Oh," Adrian said.

"Sorry for the interruption," Zoë offered.

"No big deal," Cooper replied. "I think that's what Carmen wanted anyway, right?"

"Absolutely," Carmen agreed brushing her foot against Zoë's leg underneath the table. "Any more questions before we continue?"

"I think we're good," Zoë said flashing a charming smile.

"Okay, then," Carmen stated averting her eyes from Zoë's. "Let's get back to it."

Cooper took another sip of soda, "Now, where were we?" he muttered. "Oh yeah, after John was turned down, James took him under his wing and taught him all there was to know about emergency vehicle operations. Eventually, John became one of the driving instructors at the police academy."

"Well, that makes sense," Chris interrupted obviously irritated. "We were right, Carmen."

"I know," Carmen remarked simply.

"Are you two going to explain?" Allen asked. "Or, leave us in the dark?"

"When Natalie called us about the suspect having returned to the crime scene, we immediately headed over there," Carmen replied.

"But, what we didn't know," Chris interjected, "was that the suspect somehow overheard that we were on our way."

"He has a police scanner?" Allen sighed.

"We're not sure," Carmen replied, "but it's feasible."

"This lunatic," Chris continued, "almost slammed into us trying to vacate the scene."

"If you look on page twelve," Zoë pointed out, "both Carmen's and Chris' statements involving the incident are explained."

There were a couple minutes of silence as everyone reread the report except for Carmen and Chris. "I'm sorry," Allen offered finally. "I skimmed it earlier because I didn't recognize the importance."

"Me either," Adrian admitted.

"The way to stay ahead of the game," Carmen said thoughtfully, "is to think outside the box."

"Elaborate," Cooper encouraged.

"Chris and I figured that the suspect probably had some sort of professional training by the way he handled the van," she explained. "Most people haven't had the opportunity to drive at high speeds except on the highway."

"And, as we all know by the frequent traffic accidents out there," Chris joked, "going fast in a straight line is one thing, but turning, braking, and the occasional shooting out the driver's side window is quite another."

"You're so right," Adrian chuckled.

"So, when you chase a suspect that is maneuvering his vehicle so skillfully through crowded city streets," Carmen interjected. "You need to consider the possibility that the suspect might be a former cop or military officer."

"Whatever happened to good guys being good and bad guys being bad?" Allen quizzed. "It was so much simpler that way."

"It's just the way it works out sometimes," Carmen remarked. "Alright, let's get back to the point."

Cooper tossed his empty Mountain Dew bottle into the trash can. "James stated he began seeing his son's temper flare more and more as time went by. On one particular day, he recalled seeing John yelling at a young new female recruit. When he questioned his son about the incident, John replied heatedly that she wasn't taking him seriously and that he hated women who didn't know their place."

"Sounds like our guy," Adrian muttered.

"Later," Cooper continued, "The new recruit turned up missing. After a search of the area, her body was discovered."

"Let me guess," Zoë concluded. "She had been strangled to death."

"Yes, ma'am," Cooper confirmed. "And after her death, she had been sliced open from the pelvic bone to the sternum."

"Was John ever a suspect?" Chris inquired.

"No," Cooper revealed disgustedly. "There wasn't any evidence found at the crime scene that might have connected him to it anyway."

"Go on, Cooper," Carmen encouraged checking the time on her wristwatch.

"After about three months, a new class formed at the academy. A young female recruit made a complaint about John, stating that he was following her around and making her feel uncomfortable. Of course, John denied any wrongdoing, but a report was written on the incident. When the recruit went running a few days later on one of the academy trails, an unknown assailant ambushed her from behind and attempted to strangle her."

"My God," Adrian gasped.

"Fortunately," Cooper emphasized, "she fought the assailant, but was eventually stabbed in the stomach. Two male recruits heard her screams and ran across the academy grounds to the nature trail. They observed someone running through the woods, but were not able to obtain a description.

The young female recruit survived her injury, but was unable to recall anything about the attack due to her trauma."

"James told me," Allen interrupted, "that right after that incident, John informed him that he was tired of Indiana and needed a change. So, he moved down here to Florida about two years ago and resided in Perrineville for some time."

"We contacted the Perrineville Police Department to see if they had any similar murder cases," Cooper interjected. "They reported that they had three identical murders approximately a year and a half ago where the victims were strangled, eviscerated, and had a word carved into their skin."

"Did they determine what the words meant?" Zoë questioned.

"No," Cooper replied. "They never did figure that part out."

After several seconds of silence, Allen's excitement got the better of him, "So, what do you all think about the new information?"

"This is one sick mother," Chris grumbled. "I'll be happy to throw this one in the electric chair myself."

"Where's the father now?" Zoë asked, stroking her chin thoughtfully.

"Who the hell cares?" Allen bellowed triumphantly. "We've already played that pawn."

Cooper glared at Allen and immediately answered Zoë's question, "He just moved here a couple of months ago, so he could be closer to his son."

"Why?" Zoë urged.

"How should we know?" Allen replied flatly. "That's a pretty pointless question anyway."

"That's enough!" Carmen interceded angrily. "You're way out of line and I will not tolerate this type of behavior."

"Its okay," Zoë said, defending Allen's outburst. "Emotions are just running high right now."

"It doesn't matter," Carmen reiterated sternly. "I need everyone to be level-headed. If any of you feel that you are unable to handle the job at hand, now is the time to tell me. If you think that being a loose cannon is something that the taskforce needs, now is the time to tell me. Either way, you will not be allowed to remain on the team. I'm giving everyone a fifteen minute break. Be back here at 12:55 if you can take on this assignment with your head on straight and your attitudes in check."

• • •

The room grew quiet as everyone except for Zoë and Carmen left the office. Both of them were in deep thought attempting to figure out the best way to handle the evolving situation. They realized that the cruel hard facts of the case were starting to influence the group's morale and decision-making skills. "We need to consider every angle before we go after this guy," Zoë finally declared.

Carmen cocked her head to one side and placed her hand on top of Zoë's squeezing it gently, "Tell me what's going on in that brilliant mind of yours."

Zoë looked hard at their hands entwined together. She took a deep breath and tried to push her personal feelings aside. She heard the uneasiness in her voice as she spoke. "I don't know why," she said softly, "but I think we're traveling down the wrong path."

Carmen didn't say a word, respecting Zoë's perspective on the case. "I think this guy has been keeping us in the game, giving us hints when we fall behind," Zoë reasoned. "I also think that he knew he didn't kill Chris' wife."

"Why would he do that?" Carmen encouraged.

"It's what excites him," Zoë responded. She looked at the polished hardwood doors that led out into the hallway and then looked solemnly into Carmen's eyes. "He purposely told the dispatcher about it being the Duhn's residence. Now, honey, think about it," she pressed. "Why would he do that?"

"To show us that he's in control," Carmen replied.

"Exactly," Zoë confirmed. "I think he wrote the word 'done' in last night's message to give us some help understanding the significance of the carvings on the bodies.

"I wonder. . ." Carmen thought aloud leaning back in her chair and crossing her arms in front of her chest.

"You wonder what?" Zoë asked, her voice rising in expectation of Carmen's revelation.

"I wonder if the first victim in Perrineville had the lead detectives name carved into her."

"I'll call down there after our meeting and find out," Zoë declared.

Chris and Adrian came back into the room and handed each of them some coffee. "Thank you," Carmen said quietly.

Sensing the unusual tension, Adrian bit the bullet, "What did we miss?"

• • •

Cooper and Allen strolled in at exactly 12:55 p.m. After everyone was situated back around the conference table, Carmen stood up and ran her fingers gently through her soft blonde hair. "I want to stress that John Patrick Burns is only a suspect in this case," she stated placing her hands palm down on the table.

"Yeah, right," Chris scoffed sarcastically.

"Remember that everyone is innocent until proven differently in a court of law," she reminded, ignoring Chris' negativity.

"But we have plenty of evidence," Allen stated defiantly. "Who else could have killed these women?"

"The boogeyman," Chris joked distastefully.

Carmen didn't say a word as she offered Zoë a reassuring smile before taking her seat. Zoë stood up and paced back and forth in front of the group with her hands clasped behind her back. "Right now, we are basing our opinion mostly on hearsay that is loosely supported by police reports," she recapped. "We need to remember how smart this guy really is and what his true motivations might be."

"What do you mean?" Cooper asked, cracking the protective seal around the cap of a new Mountain Dew bottle.

"Well, for one, I think the killer knew he didn't murder Chris' wife," Zoë stated blatantly. "I think he was just giving us some more clues that would help us figure out the meaning of the words on the bodies."

"You have got to be kidding," Chris replied.

"I wish I was," Zoë retorted. "I think he wrote that message at last night's crime scene to allow us to keep up with him. I don't think his main objective is killing although he does quite enjoy it. I think his main objective is to see if we are as clever as he is. And, if the killer is really John Patrick Burns, then we need to consider the possibility that his father might have informed him he's our primary suspect."

Zoë fixated her gaze on Carmen and gave a little nod of encouragement to put her two cents in. Carmen hadn't realized until that precise moment how breathtaking Zoë looked. Zoë's hair was pulled back into a ponytail allowing everyone an unobstructed view of her finely sculpted facial features. Her soft yellow dress shirt had the top two buttons undone revealing her exquisite neckline and sensational golden tan. It took all the willpower Carmen had to peel her eyes away.

"Even if it takes a little longer, let's get a search warrant prior to talking to John Burns," Carmen suggested. "We can list the variety of things we're looking for and conduct a search thorough enough of his home that even if it's a haystack we can find the needle."

"That's a good idea," Cooper complimented.

"Plus, I think we should get a hold of James and have him come down to the station," Carmen continued. "I want a sworn written statement before James has a change of heart about his son."

"We have to do this completely by the book," Zoë chimed in. "We can't make any mistakes and allow the killer to slip through our fingers because of sloppy police work."

"We need to confront John first, ask him some questions, and see how he reacts," Carmen added. "Then, we can present the search warrant and if need be, bring him back here, get his fingerprints on record, and do whatever else needs to be done."

"Do you think we have the wrong guy?" Adrian asked, sensing the skepticism in Carmen's voice.

"I just want to be sure it is the right guy," Carmen responded passionately. "I will not let our enthusiasm interfere with the proper procedures that must be taken."

"So what's our next move?" Adrian urged trying to keep her excitement from showing.

"Well, we need to have a plan," Carmen remarked.

"What the hell is there to plan?" Allen responded. "We have his address. Let's go talk to him right now and put this matter to rest once and for all."

"He isn't going to go anywhere without us knowing, remember?" Cooper interjected sharply. "I've already placed his apartment under surveillance."

"Good work," Carmen said impressed.

"Have they seen the brown van yet?" Zoë inquired.

"No, they haven't," Cooper responded, his tone thick with disappointment. "The apartment complex has individual garage units for the residents to park their cars in."

"The apartment manager advised that most of the residents leave their garage doors up when they leave and close them when they come back," Allen interjected.

"So, we're assuming that he's home?" Chris asked disapprovingly.

"I guess," Allen replied defensively.

"Jeez, will you two knock it off," Adrian growled. "Can we all just act like we're on the same team for once today?"

No one spoke and Carmen watched as her team tried to maintain their indifference. Cooper sat with his arms crossed and his hands captured underneath his armpits with only his thumbs free. His face was expressionless and his eyes focused on the half full bottle of Mountain Dew that was in front of him. Allen's left hand was massaging his temple in a rhythmic motion. His eyes were closed, but the faint sound of his teeth grinding together could be heard. Adrian was stretched back in her chair with her long athletic legs extended out in front of her. Her hands were interlaced behind her head as she leaned back and stared at the ceiling. Chris had an eerie calm about him. His thumbs were underneath his chin with the palms of his hand laid flat against each other in front of his face in a prayer like manner. He refused to look at Carmen.

Carmen and Zoë exchanged worried glances on the unsettling quiet. Carmen slipped out of her seat and took off her dress coat draping it over the back of the chair. She rested her hands on top of it and leaned forward. She waited for each one of them to look up at her. "If any of you have reason to believe that we should go over there right now without a warrant, speak now."

"We have the right guy," Chris declared impatiently. "I don't know what the hell is wrong with everyone? John Burns tried to kill my wife and, by luck, he screwed up. Nothing that anyone can dream up will change my mind about that."

"I happen to agree with him," Allen interjected.

Chris stood up and unbuttoned the top button of his dress shirt. "Allen and I are going to go obtain a search warrant from the State Attorney's Office since Carmen feels so unsure about the validity of our hard work," he hissed. "I want you, Cooper, to get a schematic of the apartment complex."

"Yes, sir," Cooper replied hesitantly.

"You two can back up Carmen on whatever else she'll need to feel safe," Chris barked, pointing his finger at Zoë and Adrian. "I refuse to sit here a minute longer and let this lunatic get another chance at killing someone else, especially my wife."

Chris stormed out of the room with Allen on his heels. Bewildered, Cooper looked at Carmen for guidance. "What do you want me to do?" he asked.

"Follow his instruction," Carmen replied firmly.

"Okay," Cooper said reluctantly. He took the final gulp of his soda and pitched it into the garbage can. He picked up his briefcase off the table and glanced at his wristwatch.

"You have plenty of time to have lunch with your wife," Carmen stated, predicting his dilemma. "It'll take a while to get the search warrant and coordinate our efforts, so we probably won't go serve the warrant until tonight."

Cooper's strained expression immediately altered into an ear-to-ear grin. Appreciatively, he couldn't resist hugging her. "Thank you," he said. "You're the best."

With that, Cooper sprinted out the door. Carmen went back to reviewing her notes. "It isn't right for Chris to be acting this way," Zoë remarked, obviously pissed off. "He's not thinking straight."

Carmen shrugged, "We all have our good days and our bad days."

"I have to agree with Zoë," Adrian said, attempting to chip away some of the hurt evident in Carmen's eyes. "I think he's a little too affected by this case for his own good."

Carmen's tough demeanor held strong. "Well, that's technically water under the bridge at this point," she said simply with a dismissive wave.

$$\bullet \ \bullet \ \bullet$$

Carmen gathered up all her paperwork and sealed it in a large yellow envelope. She placed the envelope in her briefcase and swung her dress coat over her left shoulder. She pushed her chair underneath the table and walked over to Zoë. "Are you ready to go?" she asked, running her fingers through Zoë's hair.

"Do you mind if I stay for a little while?" Zoë countered. "I just want to delve a little deeper into a few facts. Plus, I need to make that call we discussed earlier."

"I don't mind," Carmen replied, slightly disappointed. "Are you going to tell me what's on your mind?"

"Not yet," Zoë stated. "Just make sure no one gets too overzealous when they're speaking to our suspect. We still have no direct evidence linking him to the murders, just circumstantial."

"I'll make sure everything goes by the book," Carmen remarked, glancing at Adrian. "I always do."

"Let's go," Adrian urged, moving toward the open doorway.

"We'll see you later," Carmen whispered as she ran the tip of her finger across the back of Zoë's shoulders.

Zoë didn't reply. She was concentrating so hard on the report that Cooper and Allen had prepared that she didn't even notice Carmen and Adrian leave the room. When she looked a half an hour later to rest her neck muscles, she was surprised to find herself alone. She peered longingly at the open doorway. She knew Carmen would conduct the investigation with professionalism and excellence, but it was her over-emotional partner she was worried about.

At 3:15, Zoë considered calling Carmen's cell phone just to tell her that she was thinking about her, but opted against it. She knew there wasn't a moment to spare. It was imperative to the investigation and to Carmen's reputation to follow through on the task she had given herself. Besides, if her gut instinct was wrong, it was her time she was wasting, not the groups'.

CHAPTER TWELVE

It was 8:00 p.m. when Carmen and Adrian arrived at the all-night diner just off of Highway 95. The diner was approximately a mile away from John Burns' complex and a favorite hangout spot among the officers. So, it made the most sense to setup the command center there. They could conduct their covert operation without any passerby, especially their suspect, paying much attention.

Adrian drove around to the back and parked beside Chris' borrowed police cruiser. Prior to their arrival, Chris had called Carmen on her cell. He insisted that she and Adrian stop by their homes and change into the preferred attire that he was insisting everyone wore for the evening's events. Reluctantly, Carmen agreed and they stopped to change as instructed.

By the time they had reached the diner though, they were sweating profusely even with the windows down due to their abundance of apparel. Their bulletproof vests were hidden underneath dark cotton t-shirts. Their black military-style pants were tucked into their black lace-up boots with tennis shoe like soles. They looked like members of Élan's elite S.W.A.T. team as they exited Adrian's squad car.

Carmen checked the signal of her cell phone one last time before tossing it onto the passenger seat. "Still no answer from Zoë?" Adrian questioned as she rounded the front of the squad car.

"No," Carmen retorted slamming the passenger door closed. "I'm starting to get concerned."

"I wouldn't worry," Adrian stated as she walked with Carmen toward their comrades huddled around Allen's police cruiser. "She probably just hit one of the buttons and switched it to silent mode by accident."

"I hope you're right," Carmen stated.

"I am," Adrian confirmed.

"Hey guys," Cooper greeted as he strutted up to them. "We've been instructed to wear these."

"Thanks," Carmen replied, taking the combat-looking vest he handed her.

"Let me guess," Adrian quipped as she accepted the other vest Cooper was carrying. "This is mandatory too, right?"

"Yep," Cooper remarked. "So much for making our suspect feel at ease."

"You can say that again," Carmen agreed.

"Did I get the sizes right?" Cooper asked thoughtfully as he watched Carmen slip the all black vest with the word 'POLICE' written in reflective white lettering on the front and back around her shoulders.

"Mine's a little snug," Adrian informed as she pushed her shoulders forward and pulled her chest inward in order to zip up the front of the vest. "I might be a size smaller when tonight is over."

"Sorry, Adrian," Cooper offered slightly embarrassed.

"It's all good," Adrian retorted. "Do I look tougher?"

Carmen smiled, "I wouldn't mess with you."

"Me either," Cooper agreed.

"That works for me," Adrian cooed.

"Have you heard from Zoë today?" Carmen asked as she double-checked her belt to make sure she had two additional Glock 40 magazines each filled with hollow-point bullets besides the one already in her gun.

"She was still at the station the last I knew," Cooper informed. "I'm sure she'll be along any minute now."

"I hope so," Carmen replied. "She was working on something when I left her this afternoon. I wonder if she's made any headway."

"I don't know anything about that," Cooper said with a shrug. "But, I do know that Chris will rip us a new one if we continue to stand over here and talk."

"He could try," Adrian smirked, "but, he wouldn't succeed."

• • •

Carmen leaned over the hood of Allen's cruiser and studied the blueprint of John Burn's apartment complex. She knew she needed to absorb as much information as she could about this unfamiliar territory. There were various possibilities on how this night could end. If everything went well, she would serve the search warrant and question the suspect about his whereabouts on the nights of the murders. She might even be able to coax him into voluntarily coming down to the station to make a statement and allow her to fingerprint him. Of course, this would probably lead to his arrest.

Another scenario would be the suspect spraying them with bullets as they walked up to the front door. Of course, there was always the possibility no one would be home at all. In any case, she had learned to trust her gut instinct. At the moment, her gut instinct told her she would feel better if she knew what was keeping Zoë from being there.

• • •

Zoë's shoulder was aching severely as she shoved her gun into the holster tucked into her waistband. The confirmation she had been waiting on had finally been faxed and she placed it carefully into a folder that already contained new information about the case. She locked the conference room door as she left and sprinted down the corridor. She was in total panic. Sweat poured down her face in large drops of anxiety. Her heart was beating so fast it felt like it was ticking down to an explosion. She had to get to Carmen. Her life depended on it.

• • •

"Alright," Allen began. "James recommended a female be the first to try to talk to John."

"Why a female?" Carmen questioned.

"He thought that John wouldn't feel as intimidated by a woman as he would a male," Allen retorted.

"Don't you think it's a little odd that a guy who apparently has a personal hatred toward women would feel more comfortable talking to a woman?" Carmen wondered aloud.

"Here we go again," Chris interrupted irritably.

"Put a lid on it," Carmen hissed. "Or, I will pull rank."

"She has more seniority than you?" Allen asked bewildered.

"By six months," he confirmed. "I'm sorry, Carmen."

"It's alright," she replied respectfully. "We're all on edge. Let's just get back to work."

"Everyone has their handheld radios switched off, right?" he questioned without missing a beat. "I want us to only use hand signals during this operation."

"Why?" Allen pressed switching his radio off.

"Because he might have a police scanner, remember?" Adrian stated obviously irritated by Allen's ignorance.

"Oh yeah," Allen smiled sheepishly.

"We're all comfortable with the plan, right?" Chris quizzed studying their faces as each one nodded their head. "Alright then, let's get to it."

• • •

Cooper followed Carmen's exact pattern across the apartment complex. He kept close and maintained a watchful eye for the suspect. Allen stayed in step a few feet behind him with Adrian and Chris bringing up the rear. Carmen made her way over to John Burn's garage unit and waited breathlessly for the rest of the task force to join her. Cooper was at her side within seconds.

"How did you end up finding the father?" Carmen whispered.

Cooper was momentarily taken aback by the timing of the question. He attempted to put his thoughts into a complete sentence. "The police department in Indiana gave us his forwarding number," he replied softly.

"So, that's how you reached him here in Elán." Carmen remarked in a tone more questioning than not.

"No, the phone number we called first was no longer in service," he replied. "The automated recording advised us to call another number and that's when we reached him here in Elán."

"What's up?" Allen pressed as he knelt down beside them.

"I'm not sure," Cooper remarked, looking at Carmen quizzically.

"Whatever it is," Chris barked softly as he and Adrian approached, "it can wait till later to discuss it. Let's proceed, shall we?"

Carmen didn't reply as she left the dark shadows of the garage unit and hurried across the freshly watered lawn. She pressed her back firmly against the rough brick wall of the apartment building and motioned Cooper to follow. Cooper sprinted across the lawn and brushed up against her as he hugged the wall with his hand resting on his gun. Allen was the last one to leave the security of the garage unit since it had been decided that Chris and Adrian would stay hidden behind the unit unless something went terribly wrong.

"Everything alright?" Cooper whispered, sensing Carmen's hesitation.

"I don't know," Carmen replied honestly. She couldn't shake the feeling that something wasn't right. She turned her head from the objective and peered out into the darkness above the garage units.

"Let's go," Allen urged impatiently. "We're wasting time."

Carmen proceeded around the corner of the complex without a word. She hurried over to the stairwell steps with Cooper and Allen at her heels. They swiftly ascended the stairs to the fourth floor before creeping up the next flight to the fifth floor. They stepped cautiously onto the concrete landing.

Luckily, the fifth floor was empty as a slight breeze blew through the corridor. There was a sturdy metal railing on each end keeping occupants of the apartment complex from meeting an untimely demise if they stepped to close to the edge. Carmen could see the palm trees swaying lazily back and forth from the wind as she and Cooper approached the apartment designated as the suspect's.

"The first number for the suspect's father was in the Élan area code, right?" Carmen whispered as she stepped past the doorway and stationed herself on the opposing side of Cooper.

"I don't think so," Cooper replied baffled. "Why? Does it matter?"

"It might," Carmen sighed regretfully.

Allen remained within the perimeter of the stairwell covering their backs and the stairs with a shotgun in case the suspect had thought about surprising them from behind. He didn't know and didn't care what Cooper and Carmen were talking about. His harsh low voice reached their ears, "Will one of you just knock on the damn door!"

Carmen angered by the remark and repulsed by her hesitation, knocked on the door. When there was no answer, she knocked again. "John Burns, I'm Detective Moore with the Elán Police Department," she announced. "I'm out here with Officer Cooper. We would like to ask you a couple of questions that might help us clear up a matter we're investigating."

Carmen and Cooper listened intensely, but there was no response from inside. Carmen knocked on the door again and raised her voice several decibels louder. "This is Detective Moore," she declared. "Please open the door so we can talk to you."

Frustrated, Cooper raised his finger to the doorbell and pressed the small dime-size white button. Instead of hearing a buzzer, they heard a faint click. "Carmen, get back!"

Cooper shrieked. He lunged forward hitting Carmen with all his body weight, toppling them over the railing.

• • •

The flash of light, the thunderous sounds of an explosion, and instant pain washed over Allen. Pieces of the suspect's front door hit the wall inches above his head. The power of the blast, though, knocked him down the cold, unforgiving, concrete staircase. He now lay sprawled out on the fourth floor and could hear Carmen pleading, but her words were muffled.

• • •

A stream of blood ran down Cooper's forehead into his eyes. He clenched onto what was left of the metal railing with one hand. His other hand was firmly clamped around Carmen's wrist as she dangled five stories above the ground. He struggled in desperation to keep Carmen alive, but knew he couldn't hold onto her much longer. And, he wasn't sure how much longer the railing would be able to hold the weight of them both.

Carmen peered down at the ground. Her mind had already accepted the grim reality that presented itself. There was no other way around it. Her throat felt as if she had inhaled an eruptive blast of ash. Her eyes were smoldering like the volcano that had spewed the ash in the first place. Her lips tasted of blood and her head felt as if it would surely fall off if she didn't stop the hammering directly against the back of her skull. She arched back to look up at Cooper. Her wrist throbbed painfully underneath the pressure of his grip.

She knew destiny had dealt her a wild card and it was up to her whether Cooper lived or died. "Let me go!" she demanded, trying to keep the overwhelming fear she felt out of her voice.

"No way!" Cooper shrieked as the railing cut deeper into his hand.

"Let me go," Carmen ordered, as another excruciating bolt of pain flashed through her wrist. "Save yourself!"

• • •

Just a few minutes before Cooper had pressed the doorbell that activated the explosion, Zoë had turned onto Broadway Street. She was less than three blocks from the apartment complex and prayed time was on her side. As she pulled up to where Chris had positioned his borrowed police cruiser, the explosion blinded her momentarily and her ears ached from the sound of the blast. "I'm coming baby!" she hollered over the dying rumble of the explosion.

• • •

The blood from the gash on Cooper's head had eased up, but he was slowly losing his grip. The flames from the fire raging on the fifth floor was burning his hand and singeing the hair on his forearm. The metal railing was starting to buckle. "Carmen, I'm going to try to swing you to the railing," he bellowed down to her. "You only have one chance, okay?"

Carmen had no time for objection. Cooper swung her almost immediately and released his grip. Carmen barely caught the railing on the fourth floor with her left hand. Her knees struck the concrete wall with a painful thud. She managed to hold onto the railing and wrapped her right arm between the metal rods that supported the top rail. She summoned up all her remaining strength to lift her right knee onto the small concrete ledge that protruded about two inches out from the railing.

Carmen pulled herself upward using her left arm and moved her right arm up and over the railing. With this added leverage, she raised her chin above the rusty top rail and lifted her left knee onto the concrete edge. Slowly, with her every muscle twitching in exhaustion, she hoisted her body onto the railing and tumbled over onto the solid ground of the fourth floor, which was cluttered with debris.

• • •

Terrified, Zoë sprinted across the lawn. She reached the first floor stairwell at exactly the same time as Chris and Adrian. They fought their way through the frantic residents fleeing their homes. Chris and Adrian were close behind, but Zoë reached the fourth floor first. She rushed over to Carmen's limp body and dropped to her knees. She gently touched Carmen's cheek and kissed her lips softly.

• • •

Carmen lay breathless covered in dust and debris. She was in immense pain and no matter how hard she tried, she couldn't open her eyes. Familiar voices reached her ears, but she was unable to call out for help. She drifted in and out of consciousness. She felt the ground leave her. She tried to speak, but couldn't. "Please God, don't let me die," she thought.

• • •

Flames were penetrating through the ceiling above and Zoë knew that there was no time to wait for the paramedics. Fighting back tears, she lifted Carmen's body over her uninjured shoulder. She staggered to her feet and moved steadily toward the stairwell. She noticed Adrian squatting down next to Allen talking to him softly. "You have to get him off this floor, Adrian," Zoë ordered. "The ceiling is going to cave in at any moment."

• • •

Chris leaned over the fourth floor guardrail and stared helplessly up at Cooper. Cooper had both hands now clamped around the railing, but the metal was scorching the palms of his hands. To make matters worse, the rail itself was bending due to the blistering heat and the force of Cooper's weight. The stairs leading up to the fifth level were blocked by fallen concrete. Even if there was another way to get to the fifth floor, it wouldn't have made much difference. The entire floor was engulfed in flames.

"Adrian, I need you right now!" Chris hollered.

Despite Allen's pleading to not leave him, Adrian rushed to Chris' side. She leaned over the railing and peered up at Cooper dangling from the fifth floor. "My God," she gasped.

Cooper struggled to keep a hold of the railing, but the dwindling strength in his hands was no match for gravity.

His hands slipped from the railing. He tried to cry out, but his voice was swallowed up by a tsunami of fear. He was overwhelmed by the sensation of falling.

Cooper's vest jerked up hard against his neck causing him to choke. He opened his eyes and found himself suspended in mid air by the sheer determination of Chris and Adrian. Both of them had lunged out grasping for anything. Chris had managed to seize a hold of one of the nylon vest straps and Adrian had somehow snagged his right arm. Though the forces of gravity being exerted on Cooper's body weight almost dragged Chris and Adrian over the railing to their deaths, they had somehow held their footing. They pulled Cooper over the railing and onto solid ground.

Chris helped Cooper to his feet as Adrian hurried back over to Allen. Cooper curled his hands inward trying to protect the severe burns he had on them. A chunk of fiery concrete broke away from the ceiling and crashed down within inches of where Chris and Cooper were standing. "Cooper, can you make it down the stairs by yourself?" Chris demanded. "The entire ceiling is getting ready to collapse and it's going to take two of us to carry Allen down the stairs!"

Cooper looked over where Allen lay and saw Adrian unloading his shotgun placing the shells in her pants pocket. At first, he didn't understand what she was doing. But, as she placed the shotgun underneath Allen's leg, he noticed the jagged piece of bone protruding above his right knee. He continued to watch in complete fascination as Adrian slipped her S.W.A.T. vest underneath the butt of the shotgun and wrap it around Allen's thigh tightening the velcro straps for stability. Then, she removed her black t-shirt exposing her bulletproof vest and the deep purple sports bra that she was wearing. She wrapped the t-shirt around the barrel of the gun and Allen's calf and tied it into a knot finishing off the splint.

"If she can do that," Cooper managed through clenched teeth. "I can get down these stairs by myself."

• • •

As soon as they were a safe distance away, Zoë gently laid Carmen down on the wet grass. "Baby, you're going to be okay," she said softly praying that Carmen could hear her. She brushed Carmen's sweat soaked hair out of her ash-filled face and sobbed. "You have to be okay. Please, baby, for me, open your eyes."

Carmen couldn't comprehend her words, but she recognized her voice. "Zoë?" she mouthed unable to lift her eyelids.

Bending down, Zoë placed her ear next to Carmen's lips, "I'm right here, honey."

"Help me, baby," Carmen breathed, slipping back into unconsciousness.

"Help is on the way," Zoë promised. "Just hang on, sweetheart."

• • •

Zoë wiped her eyes on the sleeve of her shirt. Carmen lay on a stretcher with an oxygen mask placed securely around her mouth and nose as the paramedics made preparations for departure to the hospital. Adrian walked up behind Zoë and encircled her arms around Zoë's body from behind. Zoë's tough facade started to crumble.

"I'll drive your car to the hospital," Adrian stated resting her chin on Zoë's shoulder. "So don't argue, give me your keys, and get into the ambulance."

Zoë dug into her pocket and pulled out the set of keys. She dropped them into Adrian's open hand. Her eyes filled with tears and her body began to tremble. She turned around and collapsed into Adrian's arms. "If only I had been here a few seconds earlier," she sobbed.

"It's not your fault," Adrian soothed, watching one of the paramedics help Cooper into the back of the ambulance alongside Carmen. "Besides, Carmen needs you to be strong."

"You're right," Zoë agreed wiping her eyes. "Tears won't help her or catch the bastard who did this to her."

"Do you want me to stop by your house and bring you some fresh clothes for the morning?"

"That would be really nice of you," Zoë remarked.

"What are friends for?"

"Would you mind bringing my briefcase that's in my rental car too?" Zoë asked, pointing to a silver SUV.

"Not at all," Adrian assured, hugging Zoë one more time before heading over to where Zoë's rental was parked.

"We don't have much time to catch this guy," Zoë called out after her.

"I'll be back tonight," Adrian promised over her shoulder.

With that, Zoë climbed into the back of the ambulance. She took Carmen's hand into hers. All the way to the hospital, she spoke encouragingly to Carmen. She gently squeezed her hand and obsessively watched the monitors hooked up to her.

When the ambulance doors opened at the emergency entrance of the hospital, Zoë's sister, Linda, was waiting. She looked directly at Zoë and then at Carmen without muttering a single word, but the horrified expression on her face said enough. The paramedics gently lowered the stretcher that Carmen was on onto a rollaway bed. Linda and another E.R.

nurse wheeled Carmen through the automatic sliding glass doors and into a room for a thorough check. Another nurse helped Cooper into an adjoining room and had him lie down on a cushiony hospital mattress with crisp white sheets.

• • •

Zoë sat in the waiting room for over an hour before she unwillingly drifted off to sleep. What seemed to be a short nap was disturbed when she felt someone nudging her in the arm. She opened her eyes to find Chris and Adrian watching her. Chris handed her a steaming cup of coffee with a tired grin. She glanced at her wristwatch and noticed that it was six in the morning.

"Your sister said that Carmen is asking for you," Adrian stated trying not to wake the other people waiting for news on their loved ones.

Zoë's heart skipped a beat, "Where is she?"

"She's in room 311. Cooper and Allen are in room 313 just one door down," Adrian declared clasping her hands high above her head and stretching her sore back muscles.

"How's Allen?" Zoë prodded. "He looked pretty banged up last night."

"We haven't been able to talk to him yet," Chris replied. "Your sister instructed us that we couldn't see any of them until this morning."

"That's why we let you sleep as long as we did," Adrian interjected.

"Well, my sister is very stubborn," Zoë stated, taking a sip of the coffee. "So, we're able to see them now?"

"Yep," Chris replied.

"By the way," Adrian interrupted, "your sister told me that if she decides to work another double shift sometime in the near future, you have to be off duty."

"That sounds about right," Zoë chuckled getting to her feet. "I've never visited this hospital as much as I have in this past week."

• • •

"We thought we would go check on Allen and Cooper and give you some private time to visit," Adrian stated following Chris past Carmen's door. "We'll be back in a little while."

"Thanks." Zoë said appreciatively.

"It's the least we can do," Chris replied.

Zoë took a deep breath and pushed open the door to Carmen's room. "Baby, I'm so glad you're here!" Carmen exclaimed lowering her forkful of eggs back down to the plate.

Zoë rushed to Carmen's bedside and noticed that her right wrist was wrapped in bandages. She kissed Carmen's forehead and continued to kiss her until tears of happiness were streaming down her face. "Baby," Zoë whispered, "I can't ever lose you."

Carmen took Zoë's hand and moved it down over her heart. "I love you, Zoë," she said softly. "I just didn't want the opportunity to pass me by again."

Zoë's eyes flooded with tears, "I love you too, honey." She wrapped her arms around Carmen. "I'll love you forever," she promised.

"Forever is quite a long time," Carmen replied. "Are you sure you're up for that."

"There's only one way to find out," Zoë challenged.

"And, what would that be?" Carmen replied, holding Zoë's gaze.

"You'll have to trust me."

"I trust you," Carmen assured.

"Good," Zoë replied. "Now finish your breakfast."

"I'm just so tired," Carmen said pushing the breakfast cart away. "I'll eat more in a little while, okay?"

"Okay," Zoë relented.

Zoë pulled the covers up to Carmen's chest to keep her warm. She stroked Carmen's hair and watched over her as she slept. Her pager vibrated a short time later notifying her to call Captain Davis. She kissed Carmen softly on the lips and slipped out of the hospital room closing the door quietly behind her.

CHAPTER THIRTEEN

Carmen awoke to find her brother, Roy, standing over her. He was dressed in his crisp Navy whites, and although impressive, his uniform didn't do him justice. He stood a mere 5'8", but his continual trips to the gym earned him a rock solid physique. His hazel eyes were identical to Carmen's. They were splashed with flakes of gold that when light hit them just right made them sparkle. He wore his sun-bleached hair extremely short around his ears following military protocol.

"Hey sis, how you feeling?" he asked easing himself gently onto the edge of Carmen's hospital bed.

"Well, I've been better," Carmen chuckled, using her left hand to pat his knee reassuringly. "The emergency doctor informed me that I have a cracked wrist, a mild concussion, and that my body is suffering from extreme exhaustion, but other than that I'll be just fine."

"You were out chasing monsters again, weren't you?" he asked slyly, arching one eyebrow higher than the other.

"I hadn't seen you in a while and wanted to get your attention," Carmen replied melodramatically, placing the back of her left hand on her forehead and sighing heavily.

Roy smiled mischievously and leaned down toward her pretending to wipe a tear from his eye. "There, there, my dear sister," he teased, "I'll just go call mom."

As Roy reached for the phone, Carmen grabbed the inside of his thigh with her thumb and index finger. He cried out as she pinched a little bit of skin. "I will personally kick your ass if you touch that phone, little brother," she promised.

"Okay! Okay!" Roy pleaded playfully. Carmen released her hold on his thigh. "Damn," he continued rubbing the inside of his leg, "mom would be pissed if she knew how mean you were to me."

Carmen and Roy erupted into laughter causing the head nurse to come rushing in. She glared at Roy and checked Carmen's monitors. Satisfied that Carmen's vitals were stable, the nurse stormed out of the room. As soon as the door closed, Carmen and Roy were cracking up again.

After about an hour of visiting, Roy bent down and gave Carmen a goodbye kiss on her forehead. He scribbled his work number on a napkin and placed it in her hand tenderly. "Here's my work number just in case you need me and can't get through on my cell," he stated protectively. "Call me if you need anything."

"I will," Carmen replied as she adjusted her body into a somewhat upright position.

"You're the only sister I have," he stated. "I'd like to keep you around for awhile."

"I read you loud and clear," Carmen assured.

Roy hid his uneasiness as he left the room. But as he stood in the bustling hallway, he felt compelled to stand watch over his sister. He closed his eyes and leaned back against Carmen's closed hospital door wondering if she would be safe. Without warning, he felt someone's palm tag him in the forehead causing him to strike the back of his head on the door.

Pissed, Roy opened his eyes to find a silver badge so close to his face that with a little more effort it would have been visiting his nose hairs. He instinctively grabbed the person's arm, but stopped when he felt a gun barrel jam into his ribcage. His eyes focused in on the face holding the gun and realized that his captor was an attractive, dark-haired woman.

"Let's see some I.D.," Zoë demanded her voice shaking with harnessed rage.

"I'm Carmen's brother," Roy declared. He pulled his Navy I.D. from his shirt pocket and held it up at eye level.

Zoë scanned the I.D. and her face became flush as she read his name. "I'm sorry Mr. Moore," she attempted, removing the Glock from his ribcage. "I thought you might be someone else."

"So, who do I have to thank for protecting my sister's room so fearlessly?" Roy asked, his anger evaporating and his appreciativeness of Zoë's actions clearly noticeable.

"Detective Zoë Childers," she replied, sticking her hand out.

"Well, I was just wondering if my sister's life was in good hands," Roy remarked shaking her hand. "And, I think she is." He softly rubbed the spot where Zoë's gun had been embedded.

"Have you been in to see Carmen yet?" Zoë inquired, already guessing that he hadn't and he would soon be informing his sister of the ambush.

"Yeah, I was just on my way out," Roy replied. "But, I guess I'll be seeing more of you anyway, right?"

Zoë looked quizzically at him, "What do you mean?"

"Well, if you're the same Zoë Childers that Carmen has mentioned time and time again," Roy smirked. "I'll be seeing you at our holiday gatherings at the very least I would expect."

Roy gave Zoë a playful punch on the shoulder and walked toward the elevators. He pressed the 'down' arrow button and glanced up and down the corridor. He rushed back over to Zoë and put his mouth up to her ear. "You don't have to bring your gun to dinner," he teased, looking around nervously as if they were being spied on. "You should be safe there."

Roy turned around and disappeared behind the closing elevator doors smiling wickedly at his fun. Zoë shook her head in amusement and quietly edged open the door to Carmen's room. "Hi, baby," Carmen greeted.

"Hi, honey," Zoë replied, rushing to Carmen's side. "How are you feeling?"

"I'm feeling better," Carmen reassured. "I still feel a little weak and my head is throbbing relentlessly, but I'll live. By the way, you just missed my brother."

"I sort of ran into him," Zoë replied trying to conceal the smile creeping up on her lips, "out in the hallway."

Studying her carefully, Carmen could sense Zoë wasn't being very forthcoming with the details. "He wasn't rude to you, was he?" she questioned.

"No," Zoë laughed. "Under the circumstances, he was quite nice."

Just as Carmen was about to inquire further on Zoë's encounter with her little brother, the door to her room began to creep open. Zoë slid her hand underneath her dress coat and gripped the handle of her gun. She moved swiftly across the room and positioned herself behind the door. She grasped the door handle and yanked the door wide open causing the intruder to tumble onto the floor. "I wouldn't move if I were you," she proclaimed as she bent down to identify the unknown intruder.

"If you even think about handcuffing me Zoë, I will slam you against that wall," the woman threatened playfully.

"Adrian?" Zoë asked bewildered.

Adrian turned over and lifted herself up onto her elbows, "Have you completely lost your mind?"

Chris peered through the open doorway, attempting to sound as serious as possible, "Is it safe for me to come in?"

He and Carmen busted into laughter as Zoë helped Adrian to her feet. Zoë picked up the baseball cap that had hindered her ability to recognize Adrian from behind and brushed it off. "Sorry about that," Zoë offered, handing the cap back to Adrian.

Adrian repositioned the cap on her head with the brim of the cap just above her eyebrows. She fell into the worn recliner next to Carmen's bed and looked hard at Zoë's briefcase resting next to the base of bed. "Now would be the perfect time to fill us in on the new information you have discovered about this case, Zoë," she declared.

"What new information?" Carmen demanded excitedly.

"Take it easy," Zoë instructed. "We all agreed that you had to be a part of this whether you were in the hospital or not."

"But," Chris interjected, "only if you promise to not get all worked up."

"I promise," Carmen smiled appreciatively, turning slightly onto her side. She took another sip of water and collapsed back down onto the pillow. She pulled the covers up around her shoulders and peered through the bed's railing at Zoë. Even though she didn't feel well, she couldn't help noticing Zoë's tight fitting jeans that showed off her cute little butt.

"After you all left yesterday," Zoë began. "I did some further checking on our suspect."

"And, what did you discover?" Chris questioned shifting his body weight from one foot to the other as he leaned up against the wall.

"Well, to put it simply," Zoë stated, "we screwed up."

"What the hell do you mean?" Chris demanded. "This guy fits our profile perfectly."

"Exactly," Zoë agreed.

"Then, what's the problem?" Chris asked with his hands rolled up into fists of frustration.

"We were simply outsmarted by the real killer," Zoë explained looking at Chris and then Adrian before settling her gaze on Carmen. "Cooper said you were questioning him on how they found the father, why?"

Swallowing hard, Carmen used the cold silver metallic rail of the hospital bed to pull herself into an upright position. "I thought it was strange that a father would give up information so easily on his son," she said objectively. "And, he encouraged us to send a female officer to talk to his son when he knew women seemed to be the focal point of his rage."

"What else?" Zoë pressed.

Carmen's eyes furrowed, "I thought it was awfully coincidental that the father lived here too. And, when Cooper told me that he didn't believe the first forwarding number for John's father was in our area code, I started to get a sickening feeling in my gut."

"Well, I went back over all the information again," Zoë stated. "I realized that out of sheer desire to catch this guy, we jumped to the wrong conclusion."

"What?" Chris demanded vehemently.

Carmen sat quietly. She knew Chris was already past his boiling point. He kept purposely avoiding her eyes inferring that he blamed himself for almost causing her death as well as Cooper's and Allen's. Adrian's expression though was just as laid back as ever. She sat coolly in the recliner and returned no acknowledgement that this new information fazed her at all.

"So, what would have been the right conclusion?" Adrian inquired easily.

"Well, the answer is a little lengthy," Zoë replied.

"I have plenty of time," Carmen interjected cheerfully.

"Yes, you do," Zoë chuckled. She opened her briefcase and removed a stack of stapled packets from inside. She gave each of them a copy to follow along with as she read aloud. "I, Detective Zoë Childers, have completed a follow-up investigation of the facts in this case. It is in my professional opinion that we are not looking for John Burns. Instead, we are looking for his father, James Paul Burns."

"You're kidding?" Chris said astonished.

"I wish I was," Zoë answered.

"Holy shit," Adrian interjected. "We're going to look like idiots."

"Not if we catch him," Carmen remarked.

"And, we're going to catch this little bastard," Chris declared angrily. "Go on, Zoë."

"First, James Burns, who will be referred to as the suspect in this report, lived in Indiana for approximately 21 years. His wife perished in a house fire when his son, John, was only five years old. It was later discovered that the suspect's wife had apparently been strangled to death prior to the fire. The case was ruled unsolved and there were no suspects."

"Where was John when all of this happened?" Adrian wondered aloud.

"John was reportedly playing outside when the fire started," Zoë informed. "The fire spread rapidly through the house due to the use of an accelerant according to the fire investigator."

"It doesn't mean he didn't strangle her," Chris interjected.

"A five year old?" Adrian challenged. "I know you're still pissed that the suspect targeted your wife, but isn't that a little farfetched."

"You have a point," Chris admitted with a smile. "I've been a little wound up lately."

"Yeah," Carmen laughed, "just a little."

"Smart ass," Chris spat good-naturedly.

"I am pretty damn smart, aren't I?" Carmen challenged. "But, we can discuss that later. What else?"

"When I went back and read the police report about that incident," Zoë stated. "There was a side note that John had seen his father and mother fighting that very same day. According to John's statement given at the time, his father had come home just before noon and was mad at his mother because lunch wasn't ready. The suspect ordered John to go outside and play. A little while later, John saw his father speeding off in his squad car. When John tried to go inside to see his mother, the door was locked."

"I hate knowing where this is leading," Carmen sighed.

"After knocking on the door with no response," Zoë continued, "John got scared and went over to a friend's house to use the phone. When no one answered, his friend's mother became worried and sent John to play in her front yard with her son. She went over to the house and pounded on the front door. She noticed that the door was warm to the touch.

So, she peeked in between the curtains covering the window and saw John's mother lying on the living room floor with flames mere inches from her body. The friend's mother raced back home and called the fire department. Unfortunately, it was too late and the flames had swallowed up the house before the fire department even arrived."

"James was never questioned?" Adrian asked miffed.

"No," Zoë replied. "Since he didn't radio in to police dispatch that he had gone home for lunch, there was no record of him being there."

"And since there's no record," Carmen chimed in, "he was able make up anything he wanted on where he was at the time of the fire."

"Didn't they think it was a little strange that John claimed his father had been there?" Adrian questioned.

"There was no hard evidence to back it up," Zoë explained. "It was a child's word against an adult's. Besides that, no one would have believed that such a highly decorated cop would be capable of such a crime."

"Times sure have changed," Chris retorted. "When I was a street cop, I don't know how many times I was called into the Captain's office because a concerned citizen suspected that I was selling drugs on my lunch hour."

"Why would anyone think that?" Adrian asked bewildered.

"Because I was parked in an empty lot," Chris replied rolling his eyes. "Of course, it was the middle of the day and had they come up to my car they would have seen me eating my tuna fish sandwich and text-messaging my wife."

"Ignorance is bliss supposedly," Carmen reminded.

"Not when that ignorance lands you in front of Internal Affairs," Chris argued.

"True," Carmen agreed. "I'm sorry that we keep interrupting, Zoë."

"That's okay," Zoë said with a smile. "After the suspect collected his wife's insurance policy, he placed John in a private school. John spent the rest of his school years visiting his father only in the summer. The suspect resigned from the force about 9 years later and went on to apply for a driving instructor position. On John's fifteenth birthday, the suspect was hired by the police academy in Indiana to teach new recruits how to drive their squad cars in emergency situations at very high speeds."

"This is still all circumstantial," Chris stated in defeat. "We can't arrest someone without proof."

Zoë looked up from her report. She reached over and took a sip of Carmen's water. She cleared her throat and rummaged inside her briefcase. "Up to this point, I have to agree with you," she admitted. "However, when I inquired about him at his old department, the few officers still left that hadn't retired, painted quite a different picture. Their recollections of our suspect consisted of allegations of robbery, rape, and an unusual circumstance where a young hooker was found strangled and stabbed with the suspect's business card in her coat pocket."

"When did James finally resign?" Carmen questioned.

"Right after the hooker was discovered," Zoë replied.

"This report still doesn't tell us anything that we don't already know," Chris said, obviously irritated. "Everything is still circumstantial and inconclusive." Stressed out, he eyed Zoë coldly, "You can't tell me that this is all you have. Are you crazy? I would expect more from you than the assumption that the father is the killer. Which one is it Zoë? They both seem just as guilty."

Stunned by Chris' outburst, Zoë sat quietly, trying to gather her thoughts. Carmen glared at Chris and for the first time during their friendship she wanted to kick Chris so hard in the groin that he wouldn't be able to make love to his wife for a year. As Chris turned to leave, Zoë gritted her teeth and growled, "John couldn't have committed these crimes, at least the ones here, he wasn't able to."

Chris stopped abruptly and spun on his heels. Carmen and Adrian exchanged confused glances, but remained silent. Chris shoved his hands deep into his pockets and leaned his body up against the right side of the doorframe. Looking at Zoë, he sighed heavily, "Why wasn't he able to?"

Zoë had been pushed to the limit and hissed, "Because you egotistical asshole, John Burns was in a car accident in Perrineville that resulted in severe brain damage and paralysis from the neck down."

"What are you saying?" Chris questioned as exhaustion corrupted his ability to comprehend.

"Basically, John is a vegetable with machines that keep his heart and lungs working," Zoë hissed. "Furthermore, his body was found in the apartment last night charred to an almost unrecognizable degree."

Chris tried to maintain his composure. "I'm sorry Zoë," he offered, his voice faltering. "I don't know what my problem is lately. I feel like I'm suffering from P.M.S. My mood is swinging across a spectrum the size of the Milky Way."

"You're forgiven," Zoë countered evenly. "But, take some Midol or something. These mood swings of yours are irritating the piss out of me."

The four of them laughed. Zoë pulled the piece of paper from her briefcase that she had been searching for. "By the way, I found out how our suspect was making a living."

"Out with it woman!" Adrian cried.

"Well, not only did he work for a flower shop in Perrineville, but he was also working for one here in Élan,"

Zoë revealed. "The shop is just down the road from the police station, but he quit two days ago."

"Let me guess," Carmen predicted. "All of the victims were customers."

"Yes," Zoë stated eyeing Chris evenly. "Do you all want me to continue?"

Chris squatted down on the floor. For the first time since his wife's life was put in danger, he listened as a detective and not a husband. Adrian and Carmen remained quiet as this silent battle between Zoë and Chris finally came to an end. Chris removed a pocketsize notebook from his back pocket. Flipping it open, he looked at Zoë respectfully, "Let's have it."

Zoë's eyes danced with excitement. "Well, first of all, the suspect also went to Indiana University. I was able to get in touch with the suspect's mother using the information forwarded to me by the police academy in Indiana. After briefing her on our situation, she informed me that she had given the suspect a gold bracelet for his graduation present. The bracelet was engraved with his initials and his university's insignia."

"Once her son is arrested," Carmen interrupted. "How can we be sure she'll testify to that?"

"I had an officer in her hometown stop by. She wrote out a sworn affidavit," Zoë replied proudly. "I received a copy of it by fax last night."

"There are still a lot of loose ends to tie up," Adrian reminded the group cautiously.

Zoë scanned her notes, summarizing as much information as possible. Carmen strained to keep her eyes open, but she was losing her battle against the effects of her pain medicine. She took the last sip of water left in her glass. She could feel herself nodding off. In desperation, she took an ice chip from the small Styrofoam bucket on the cart next to her bed and rubbed it all over her face.

Zoë noticed Carmen's struggle. "I want to run through the rest of these facts as quickly as possible," she said. "We don't have a lot of time to spare."

Adrian and Chris answered her by their silence as they both helplessly watched Carmen fight to stay awake. "The crime scene team located the van registered to John Burns in the garage unit assigned to his apartment," Zoë began. "On the dash, they recovered the suspect's license. A serrated knife was taped up underneath the driver's seat and a surgical scalpel was discovered in the glove compartment. There were traces of blood found on the knife and scalpel. Both have been sent to the crime lab for DNA testing. Furthermore, the brown fibers found at the first crime scene are a match to the van's interior carpet."

"He's going to run," Carmen muttered through her sleepiness. "What we need to do is figure out where."

"Well, I thought about the message he left at the crime scene and the significance of the third letter missing in each carving," Zoë replied. "Then, I called the police department in Perrineville and they faxed me copies of the case files on their murders."

"You figured it out, didn't you?" Adrian asked excitedly.

"Well, Carmen and I were on the right track," Zoë announced confidently glancing down at her notes. "The first victim was murdered in the same neighborhood that the lead homicide detective for Perrineville resided in. The second victim was murdered approximately five miles away from another officer's home."

"And, the third victim," Carmen guessed, her words slightly slurred, "was reported as one of the investigator's wives."

"Exactly," Zoë answered, turned on by Carmen's determination to withstand the effects of the pain medication.

"The words that were etched into the victims in Perrineville," Adrian inquired eagerly, leaning forward so her elbows rested on the top of her knees. "Were they determined to be officers' names as well?"

"Yes," Zoë answered without hesitation. "But, their investigators didn't realize it until we had compared notes."

"So," Chris began his tone professional and courteous but full of anticipation. "What have you put together?"

Rubbing the palms of her hands together, Zoë's eyes darted down the page of her notes. "The first victim in Perrineville was engraved with the word 'than'," she reported. "This, at first didn't seem to make any sense until I learned the lead investigator's name." Zoë looked at Chris and Adrian, her eyes sparkling, "His name is Detective Ethan Hunter."

"You have got to be kidding," Adrian declared. "The killer didn't change his modus operandi at all?"

"Except instead of using our first names, he used our last names," Carmen replied.

"Why?" Chris pondered aloud.

"Because yours, Carmen's, and Cooper's first names wouldn't work in his plan," Zoë replied. "The first victim as I said was missing the 'E' for Ethan. The next victim had the word 'inn' cut into the pelvic region. The female officer assisting with the investigation was Linn Peters. The final victim had the word 'ate' carved into her. This one threw me at first, because I initially thought it was relating to the number eight. But, as I finished reading the report, I realized that the investigator who signed it was Nathan Drake."

"Holy Shit!" Chris exclaimed. "The short for Nathan is Nate, but what made you think of that?"

"Well, I didn't at first," Zoë replied honestly. "I called the police department and asked to speak with him. When he picked up the phone, he greeted me by saying, 'This is Nate. How may I help you?' After talking to him for a little while, he informed me that he is rarely called Nathan and they always print his name in the paper as Nate Drake."

"I bet you almost fell out of your chair," Chris stated.

"Well," Zoë began, taking a deep breath and exhaling slowly. "I just about did when I figured out the rest of it."

"What do you mean?" Adrian inquired over the noise of her stomach grumbling for food.

"You see," Zoë explained. "I knew there had to be a reason why our suspect decided to start using last names instead of continuing to use first names. So, on a piece of paper I wrote down each of the missing letters from the words on the bodies in Perrineville, E-L-N. Then I wrote out the letters missing on the victims here, O-H-O."

"I still don't understand," Adrian remarked, visibly confused.

"I didn't either at first," Zoë acknowledged. "But, then I remembered that the suspect had been a cop. So, what would be the significance in leaving out certain letters in people's names? Was he playing some sort of sick twisted mind game with us? He wasn't insane, he knew what he was doing was wrong. As I struggled to understand his motive, I started to think about the significance in choosing the lead homicide detectives' residences to start his killing spree."

"And?" Chris insisted eagerly.

"The letters E-L-N were purposely left off on the victim's in Perrineville so if the detectives were smart enough they would be able to discover the killer's next move. But, he wasn't going to hand it to them, so he gave them clues. The problem was that the clues were only obvious to the killer because he hadn't given the detectives there enough to go on."

"You're saying that he wanted to see if the police could catch him," Adrian stated disbelievingly.

"Yep," Zoë confirmed.

"That's messed up," Chris chimed in.

"It sure is," Zoë agreed. She walked over to the hospital window and twisted the rod hanging from the top of the blinds, opening them slightly. The warmth radiating through the window from the midday sun felt good on her face. She moved back around to the front of Carmen's bed and paced back and forth. "The suspect took the promotional test to become a detective 6 times according to his service record," she relayed in a monotone voice. "He failed 5 out of those 6 times. When he did finally pass the exam, he lost the position to another officer who out scored him considerably."

"And, what he so desperately thought he deserved," Carmen interjected groggily.

"Was the one thing he couldn't kill to get," Zoë finished.

"Which was?" Adrian questioned.

"To be a detective," Carmen answered.

"I think that was what pushed him over the edge, so to speak," Zoë concluded, brushing a strand of hair away from her right eye. "And, guess what?"

"What?" Chris challenged as he combed back his feathery hair.

"The person who beat his score on the detective's exam was a woman," Zoë replied.

"Wow!" Adrian exclaimed, goose bumps forming on her thighs. "But, that still doesn't tell me what the missing letters mean?"

"E-L-N is a word that is also missing a letter," Zoë responded flatly.

"It's the 'a' in Élan," Carmen gasped. "The suspect was telling them that he was coming here."

Adrian and Chris looked at each other in amazement. Zoë smiled with pride as Carmen pushed herself up onto her elbows with the last bit of her strength. "O-H-O is missing the letter 'I'," Carmen continued. "The suspect is planning on going to Ohio next."

Chris sprang to his feet acknowledging his partner's revelation, "Zoë? Is Carmen right?"

Zoë leaned over Carmen and ran her fingers through Carmen's soft hair. "Yeah, she's right," she replied. "I called the bus station and the airport in hopes that he bought a ticket registered under his name."

"Did he?" Adrian pressed.

"No," she answered simply.

"Damn it all to hell!" Chris growled, attempting to keep his voice low to avoid disturbing Carmen, who was completely passed out.

Zoë slipped on her black leather jacket and motioned Adrian and Chris into the hallway. She led them into an empty waiting room. "What's interesting," Zoë revealed, "is that John Burns shows up on the passenger manifest on a flight from here to Ohio that leaves tonight at 10:35 p.m."

"Awesome!" Chris cried out.

"We have to be careful," Zoë warned. "He probably thinks we haven't figured it all out yet, but he'll still be watching out for us."

"What if he talks to his mother and realizes we're on to him?" Adrian asked inquisitively.

"I don't think that will be a problem since she just found out her grandson was killed in last night's explosion."

"Let's go get an early dinner and make plans for this evening," Adrian suggested.

"You two go ahead," Zoë urged. "I'm going to eat in the cafeteria and stay with Carmen for as long as possible. Besides, I want to fill her in on what's going down tonight when she wakes up."

"Do you want to meet at the station around seven o'clock?" Chris offered.

"Sure, that's perfect," Zoë replied.

"Alright then," Chris remarked, "we'll see you later."

As Chris and Adrian turned to leave the waiting room, Zoë called after them, "I forgot to tell you one other piece of information I learned."

"Which is?" Chris replied.

"The lead investigator in Perrineville was shot in the neck while sitting at a stoplight. The bullet passed through his neck barely missing his jugular."

"Did he make it?" Adrian asked.

"He's okay now, but it put him in intensive care for a while," Zoë informed. "So when we nab this guy, we need to be really careful. Remember, he has nothing to lose."

CHAPTER FOURTEEN

When Carmen awoke, the last rays of light were retracting through the small slits between the blinds. She pressed the button on her bed remote for the nurse. Within minutes, a slender woman with strawberry colored hair appeared in the doorway. "What is it that you need, dear?" she asked kindly.

"Could you turn the overhead light on for me?" Carmen inquired. "And, I'm a little hungry."

"No problem at all," the nurse replied with a smile. She switched on the light and bounded out the door.

Carmen carefully maneuvered herself onto her side. She reached for the phone beside her on the small round table positioned next to the bed. She noticed a note addressed to her from Zoë taped to the receiver. It read:

> We're on our way to the airport to arrest the
> suspect. I left my notes inside your briefcase
> beside the bed.   ~love you, Zoë

Carmen reached down blindly and brushed the handle of her briefcase. She slipped her fingers underneath the handle and painfully lifted it onto her lap. The gold metal snaps popped loudly as she pressed the release buttons. She pulled Zoë's reports out and began scanning the information.

The nurse entered five minutes later with dinner. Carmen picked at her food and occasionally took bites of the gravy-smothered turkey. She soon was moving on to her blue Jell-O. As the last bite fell into her mouth, her eyes locked in on James' flight information. She glanced at the clock noting the time. His flight would be taking off in an hour and forty minutes. Without hesitation, she reached for the phone. There was no way she was going to miss this.

• • •

The hospital room door edged open and a sliver of light from the nurse's station seeped into the room. Roy slipped in like a thief in the night with a giant duffel bag and clicked the door shut. "You ready?" he whispered.

"Yeah, of course," Carmen replied. She eased out of the shadows and walked stiffly toward him. She was dressed in the clothes Zoë had left for her. The black sweatpants, although quite large, allowed her aching body some comfort and the white cotton t-shirt covered her bruised stomach. Her left hand clenched the collar of her leather coat as she lazily dragged it on the floor behind her.

Roy unzipped the duffle bag and removed Carmen's bulletproof vest that he had taken the liberty to clean up after the explosion. He helped her slip it on over her head and adjust the velcro straps for a secure fit around her chest. He placed her tennis shoes down in front of her and helped her balance as she put them on.

"I'll tie them if you want," he offered.

"That would be nice," she replied frustrated by the limited use of her right hand.

Roy knelt down and double-knotted the laces of the tennis shoes. Carmen carefully maneuvered her right arm into the sleeve of the leather jacket. "Can you tell I'm wearing a vest?" she inquired after zipping up the front.

"Not really," Roy remarked, digging through the duffle bag again.

"What are you looking for?" Carmen prodded.

"The box of hollow-point bullets that I brought with me," he explained.

"Where did you find hollow-point bullets?"

"In your closet," he whispered. "Chris unloaded your gun earlier because he didn't think it was very safe to have it lying around the hospital unattended. He took the unspent bullets and tucked them into his pants pocket. Your gun is completely empty."

"How do you know that?" Carmen pressed.

"Because Chris called me around eight o'clock and told me," Roy revealed.

"Where is my gun now?" Carmen asked worriedly.

"Chris told me that he tucked it in between the mattresses of your hospital bed," Roy replied.

Carmen ran her left hand between the two mattresses. "Found it," she softly exclaimed.

"Here you go," Roy encouraged handing Carmen the first of fifteen hollow-point bullets.

"Thanks," she replied pressing the release for the magazine. She pulled back the slide and double-checked it to ensure there wasn't a bullet in the chamber.

• • •

Roy looked up and down the hallway to make sure the coast was clear. He strutted over to the elevator and pressed the down button. He watched the numbers above the elevator entryway light up as it ascended past the other floors. When the elevator doors opened, he scanned the hallway one more time before motioning Carmen to come.

Carmen slipped out of the hospital room, tiptoed across the hall, and slid into the elevator. Roy selected the first floor and pressed the button for the doors to close. As they descended, Carmen informed Roy exactly where they were headed and what she was up to.

"So," Roy began when Carmen finished, "I just helped you escape from a hospital room where you should be resting."

"Yes," she confirmed.

"And now we're headed to the airport, so we can guarantee the capture of a serial killer?" he added, shaking his head in disbelief.

Smiling wickedly, Carmen squeezed his hand. "Come on," she coaxed. "This is just like when we used to play cops and robbers as kids."

"There's just one big difference," Roy replied sarcastically, amazed at the degree he would entertain Carmen's wishes. "There were never real bullets in our guns."

• • •

Out in the hospital parking lot, Carmen climbed on the back of Roy's midnight blue Ninja motorcycle. She tucked her injured wrist between their bodies for stability and wrapped her other arm around Roy's waist. Roy started the engine and Carmen hugged her aching thigh muscles around the cycle for added support. She nuzzled her head into the back of his brown leather bomber jacket inhaling the familiar scent of his cologne.

204 ∞ D.C. ELMORE

Roy eased the motorcycle carefully out of the parking lot into traffic and picked up speed gradually as he attempted to keep Carmen as comfortable as possible. He maneuvered skillfully through the side streets, beating red lights and avoiding unrelenting intervention by street cops. He knew all to well that they would pull him over if they weren't busy with another call.

Until he bought his motorcycle, Roy couldn't relate at all to the discrimination Carmen had to contend with on a daily basis. But, he began getting a small taste of it every so often from the local beach cops. He had been stopped numerous times while driving his motorcycle. Each time, regardless of the officer's viewpoint, he had been doing the speed limit and driving defensively. Although he had never been given a traffic citation, it didn't stop the officer from trying to provoke him. Usually the officer would criticize the Navy and refer to the sailors as alcoholics and rough necks wasting precious tax dollars.

In the Navy, Roy had to comply with certain polices that civilians didn't have to abide by. One such policy was that all military personnel had to wear a bright orange vest when riding a motorcycle on the naval base. Most of the enlistees wore their vests whenever they were out and about on their motorcycles just in case they were called into work. Each time Roy or, for that matter, other friends of his in the Navy had been pulled over, they had been wearing a vest.

Roy eventually talked to Carmen about the unjust treatment he was receiving. Carmen used her position at the department and took it up with a couple of the Captains over in the traffic division. She informed them that there were numerous complaints coming in about officers stopping Navy personnel without cause. The Captains brought it to the suspected road officers' attention and reiterated that to pull a motorist over they must have a justifiable reason to do so. If not, it was basically false arrest. Unfortunately, Roy had been pulled over three more times since then. On the flipside, two of the officers were now under investigation by the Department of Internal Affairs.

Carmen peered over Roy's shoulder and embraced the wind as it whipped through her hair. She strained to keep her eyes open as they started to water. Roy's helmet felt cool against her left cheek and helped ease her throbbing headache. "I love this!" she shouted squeezing his waist gently.

"It's as close to flying as you can get on wheels," Roy yelled back.

They turned onto I-95 North and within minutes were taking the exit ramp onto the Airport's expressway. Roy downshifted as they approached the drop-off area for passengers and eased over the vicious speed bumps that would cause an unskilled rider to get an up close and personal look at the pavement. Roy maneuvered between two taxis and brought the bike to a complete stop. A young man in black slacks and a white uniform shirt approached them as Carmen climbed off the back of the motorcycle.

"I'm sorry, but you can't park here," he said, eyeing them suspiciously.

"Yes, we can," Carmen insisted, reaching into her jacket pocket for her badge. "I'm a cop."

"Sure you are," the young man replied sarcastically.

"She is," Roy barked.

"I don't care if you believe that she's Santa Claus," the young man spat disrespectfully. "I will have it towed."

"No, you won't," Carmen interrupted bringing her identification and badge to the young man's eye level. "In fact, you're going to stand here and make sure it doesn't get towed. Understand?"

"Yes, ma'am," he replied. "I'm sorry, Detective Moore. I'm just doing my job."

"Here's something I've learned," Carmen offered. "If you want respect, you have to earn it."

"Yes, ma'am."

Carmen glanced down at her watch. "It's 10:15 p.m." she announced. "The suspect's plane takes of in twenty minutes."

"What suspect?" the young man prodded.

"Don't you think he's probably been apprehended by now?" Roy asked as both of them ignored the question.

"Possibly," Carmen replied pulling a knitted hat out of her coat pocket and fitting it onto her head. "But, there's only one way to be sure."

"What's going on?" the young man demanded. "Can I help?"

"I'm putting you in charge of making sure nothing happens to this motorcycle," Carmen instructed. "Can you handle that?"

"Absolutely!"

"Let's go," Carmen exclaimed tucking her badge back inside her pocket. She grabbed a hold of Roy's arm and they walked into the Elán airport pretending to be a couple.

"By the way," Roy began as they passed by the ticket counters. "How did this guy get through security?"

"Well, according to the information that Zoë left," Carmen replied. "It's possible that our suspect is representing himself as a U.S. Marshall using his son's name."

"I understand why he would lie about his name," Roy remarked. "But, why about being a U.S. Marshall?"

"You can't get through security with a gun, otherwise," Carmen reminded. "And, I'd bet money that he has a gun."

Carmen removed her identification and badge from her jacket. She and Roy made their way through the crowded line of travelers. She approached the officer standing in front of the security checkpoint station refusing to allow anyone through to their gate. "I'm Detective Moore with the Élan police department," she whispered handing him her identification. "I'm sure you have been alerted to the situation at hand."

"Yes, ma'am," he answered. "I'm under orders not to let anyone through. You can see what kind of impact that is having."

"Have they apprehended the suspect?" Carmen pressed.

"Not to my knowledge."

"Why wasn't there an order to stop him at the security check point?" Carmen inquired her ears picking up on a distant commotion.

"The suspect had checked in early apparently," the security guard replied. "So, when we were alerted to be on the look out for him it was a little too late."

Gunfire erupted interrupting their conversation. "Get down!" Carmen shouted. "Everyone get down!"

Some of the travelers dropped their baggage and took off running in every direction imaginable except toward where the gun shots had originated from. Some screamed for help while others added to the chaos by bellowing that terrorists were taking siege of the airport. A few travelers were paralyzed by fear and resembled the hard plastic ducks with bull's-eyes on them at the small town carnivals. A good number, though, obeyed Carmen's orders and flattened their bodies against the worn airport carpeting.

Carmen had instantly dropped to one knee and dragged Roy down behind her. She removed the Glock from her holster and crawled to the very front of the x-ray machine for cover. James Burns barreled toward the security checkpoint in a flat-out run shooting wildly behind him. She would have a perfect shot in a matter of seconds.

James released the empty magazine from his gun and discarded it onto the floor. He quickly jammed another one in its place. Carmen took a deep breath and leveled her gun. But, as she lined up the sights, her heart plummeted to the pit of her stomach where torment lies in wait. Chris and Zoë were directly behind him running in a criss-crossing pattern attempting to gain ground and avoid a deadly rendezvous with a bullet to the chest at the same time. If she pulled the trigger and missed the suspect, she would surely strike one of them. And although she was usually an expert shot, she knew she was still under the heavy influence of the pain medication.

"Shoot him," Roy encouraged softly.

"I can't," Carmen replied dropping back out of sight. "If I miss him, I might hit Zoë or Chris and the suspect will know where I am. If he starts shooting over here, an innocent person might be hurt or killed."

"What are you going to do?" Roy asked alarmed. "He'll be on top of us in just a few seconds."

"Just stay quiet," she instructed.

James continued to fire wildly behind him as he passed by where Carmen and Roy were hiding. He sprinted toward the down escalator without giving the terrified travelers a second glance. Carmen grasped the opportunity and rolled underneath the conveyor belt. She sighted in on the suspect's leg as he stepped onto the metal platform of the escalator and squeezed the trigger. James shrieked in pain and grabbed his left thigh as the bullet tore threw the muscle surrounding his femur. He tried to turn and shoot, but tumbled headfirst down the escalator.

Stunned, Chris and Zoë stopped in their tracks and scanned the area for the second shooter. "It's alright," Carmen shouted out to them. "It's just me."

Zoë rushed over to her, "What in the hell are you doing here?"

"I had to be here," Carmen attempted. "I thought I might be of some use."

"You stay right here until this whole thing is over," Zoë ordered worriedly. "I'll come get you when we have him in custody and you can read him his rights."

"Okay," Carmen replied with a shrug.

Zoë left the comfort of protection behind the conveyor belt. She nodded to Chris that she was ready and they took positions on both sides of the escalator. Chris quickly looked down the moving staircase to make sure it was safe to follow. Zoë noticed a splatter of blood running down the smooth silver surface of the escalator sidewall.

"Let's go," Chris declared. He and Zoë descended the escalator without looking back.

Carmen sat still, straining to hear the cries of triumph from a successful capture. But the only sounds her ears could decipher were the residual panic still coming from down the corridor. She turned to Roy, the intensity of her words burned into him. "Check down there," she instructed, pointing toward the airport terminal. "Adrian was supposed to have been with them."

Roy nodded his head in agreement. He had never been witness to an actual shooting even after all his years in the Navy. "Watch your back," he urged.

"I always do," Carmen replied reassuringly before turning to the security guard. "Go with him."

"What?" the guard asked, his voice slightly cracking.

"You heard me," Carmen commanded.

With that, she proceeded to the escalator and squatted down next to it. She stepped onto the revolving steps and rode down into the unknown, making sure that no part of her body was visible above the handrails. She eased onto the bottom platform and backed herself up against one of the side walls for cover. She could hear harsh voices and she shifted onto her stomach and curled her legs up behind her so that they would not be nicked by the revolving staircase.

Carmen noticed a small group of people huddled behind a rental car company counter for protection. They spotted her easily from their vantage point, but were careful not to make any sounds that would alert either arguing party of their presence. Carmen inched her way forward on her knees and elbows until she could see the situation at hand. James was leaning against a pillar about twenty feet away for support with the muzzle of his gun pressed firmly against Chris' left temple. Zoë had her gun raised to the suspect's eye level. She was desperately trying to talk him into putting the gun down and accepting a more peaceful resolution. Carmen shifted restlessly trying to gain a good position to take James out if it came down to it.

"If you don't put that fucking gun down, I swear I'll blow his head off!" James shrieked. "It won't matter if you shoot me! You will still be one cop short!"

"Okay! Okay!" Zoë finally agreed knowing there was no way out. The more she talked to him the more agitated he became. Surely, if he turned the gun on her, Chris would attack him, wouldn't he?

Carmen remained hidden behind the escalator wall, horrified by the events unfolding in front of her. "Don't do it, Zoë," she pleaded silently. "He'll kill you both once you're disarmed."

Zoë lowered her weapon and bent down slowly. She allowed the gun to slip from her fingers and onto the ground. The suspect removed the gun from Chris' temple and pointed the barrel directly at Zoë as she stood back up. Zoë's face drained of color as she realized destiny's cruel twist of fate. Chris, paralyzed by fear, couldn't move. The suspect's finger tightened on the trigger and three gunshots pierced the air almost simultaneously.

• • •

Zoë cowered on the ground with her arms shielding her face and head. Glass showered down over her from the shattered wall-length window behind her. The echoes of gunshots rang in her ears followed by an unexpected silence. She strained to hear the suspect's voice, but all was still. She cautiously peeked through her hands still afraid she would be looking down the barrel of a gun.

She saw Chris kneeling down beside James. She moved her hands away from her head and patted her body down for any bullet holes. Overjoyed to find herself still in one piece, she shifted her attention back to James sprawled out on the floor. A dark reddish puddle had begun to form underneath his head. Her attention was immediately averted to Carmen struggling to her feet from behind the solid escalator wall assisted by one of the Élan S.W.A.T. team members that had descended the escalator's steps.

• • •

Carmen yearned to wrap her arms around Zoë and cover her face in kisses, but she had to focus on the work that needed to be done. Once the crime scene had been secured, she ambled over to the suspect's body and peered down at the gaping holes in the side of his head. She had never shot anyone before tonight and her hands were still trembling. She closed her eyes and said a quiet prayer for the families of the victims and the suspect.

Debra snapped a few more shots of the body before moving over to take some close-up pictures of the spent shells. Chris squatted down next to Carmen and began searching James' pockets. Carmen desperately wanted to help in the collection of the evidence, but she wasn't feeling at all well. Her wrist throbbed painfully, her headache was on the brink of a migraine, and she was desperately trying to maintain her composure knowing she had almost lost the woman she loved. She tried valiantly not to look at Zoë, but she couldn't resist. She stared hopelessly at her lover and watched as Captain Davis recorded Zoë's statement about the events that had just transpired on audiotape.

Carmen's eyes were brimming with tears when Chris removed a small notebook from the inside pocket of James' jacket. She pulled her eyes from Zoë's body and studied the pages of the notebook as Chris flipped through them. Carmen was appalled and outraged by its content. Page after page, James described how he flirted with each of the victims at the flower shop and then followed them to learn their routines. In addition, he had created a chart listing the neighbors of each victim and what time they came home in the evening.

In the section related to the first victim, James had Carmen's name highlighted in bright yellow with the word 'detective' beside it. He had noted the approximate times she walked Cuffs. In the margin, he had scribbled down the make, model, and color of her car including the license plate number. The following pages contained similar information on the other two victims. The second victim, Ms. Lopez, had five pages dedicated to her daily rituals including the exact time she went out every night to pull her BMW into the garage. Chris' home address was written down on the top of the page that described the third victim's daily activities. The approximate time the victim would be coming home from work the day she was murdered was also noted.

On some of the pages, James made reference to the women's bodies and listed in graphic detail what he wanted to do to them. He jotted down little messages referring to women's self-righteous spirits needing to be broken. Chris' eyes furrowed in the deepest kind of hatred when he read a little synopsis about James watching his wife plant flowers in the yard and how good it would feel to kill her, knowing it was the wife of a detective trying to catch him.

Chris flipped to the very last page of the notebook. "Look at this, Carmen," he said obviously disturbed.

Carmen peered down at the notebook, "This is unreal."

They stared at each other in amazement. In their grasps were all the victim's names and the dates of their deaths starting with the recruit found slain at the police academy in Indiana, Lisa Scott. Carmen swallowed hard as she saw her own name neatly handwritten in the last space dedicated to the victims he had murdered in Élan. Beneath her name, a thick line from a pencil had been drawn across the entire page. A new list had been started with a number one inserted on an empty line.

"Jeez," Chris gasped. "He had already started planning for his next victim."

"He was one sick son of a bitch," Carmen agreed, choking back the lump she felt rising in the back of her throat.

"Hey!" Adrian shouted exuberantly.

Carmen spun around and smiled triumphantly as Roy and Adrian stepped off the escalator and strutted over to where they were standing. Roy placed his arm around Carmen's shoulder and squeezed her gently. "I'm glad you're okay," he whispered.

"Me too," she replied, leaning into him slightly.

"How are you holding up?" Roy prodded.

"Truthfully," Carmen retorted, "I feel terrible."

"Let's get you home," he said softly.

"That's a good idea," Chris encouraged, dropping James' notebook into an evidence bag and sealing the opening with translucent red tape.

"Give that evidence to Sgt. Hammond," Captain Davis interrupted striding up to them with Zoë at his side. "You are all off duty as of right now."

"But Captain. . ." Carmen protested.

"Aren't you supposed to be in the hospital?" Captain Davis reminded, attempting to hide how proud he was of her. Without waiting for an excuse, he continued brusquely, "I expect individual reports from each of you on my desk sometime tomorrow even if you fax them from your home."

"Will do," Carmen said.

Chris handed Sgt. Hammond the evidence bag and peeled off his latex glove. He tossed them into a round trash container before shaking Roy's hand. "Well, it's nice to finally meet you," he greeted. "I never thought the circumstances would be quite like this though."

"Same here," Roy replied, adding a little more firmness to his handshake.

Captain Davis leaned over and whispered into Zoë's ear. Zoë smiled and nodded her head in agreement. He patted her on the back and walked away. Carmen looked quizzically at her, but Zoë just brushed her off, "Tell ya later."

• • •

Adrian and Roy chatted up a storm as the five ascended the escalators. "When I found Adrian," he relayed excitedly, "she was giving CPR to an old man who had suffered a heart attack after the first shot rang out."

"Really?" Carmen remarked, listening earnestly.

"Yeah," Adrian interjected. "Poor guy was completely terrified."

"That's terrible," Zoë chimed in. "How is he now?"

"He's going to make it," Roy replied, "thanks to Adrian."

"Don't be so modest," Adrian interrupted, turning to Carmen. "Your brother did the chest compressions while I performed mouth-to-mouth."

"I'm so proud of both of you," Carmen replied.

"Are you going to tell me what happened with you all?" Roy inquired.

Carmen slipped her hand into Roy's and remained silent as they walked through the exit doors. The cool night breeze seized the warmth from her skin. "You'll have to ask them," she finally stated, nodding her head in the direction of Chris and Zoë.

"This is the short version," Zoë began. "We thought that after the suspect had fallen down the escalator, he would either be out of commission or would flee toward one of the doors leading to where the shuttle vans are parked."

"We were wrong," Chris grumbled flatly.

"When I reached the bottom of the escalator, I didn't see him," Zoë stated regretfully. "So, I took off toward the exit."

"I started to run after her," Chris interjected, shaking his head in disbelief that what followed next really happened. "But, that stupid son of a bitch was hiding behind one of the pillars."

"Came up right behind him and placed a gun to his head," Zoë finished.

Chris acted out the scene by placing his left index finger to his head and raising his thumb to act like a trigger. Zoë looked away with a shudder. Adrian unable to resist, urged them on, "What happened next?"

"I looked back at Chris at the exact same time James came up behind him," Zoë recalled disheartened, patting her holster with her right hand. "I yanked my Glock out about the same time James put his gun to Chris' head."

Engrossed in the story, Roy unintentionally stepped off the curb. He fumbled for his keys inside his leather jacket slightly embarrassed. "Come on, you can't leave us hanging," he encouraged, noticing Adrian was taking an extreme interest in his motorcycle.

"Well," Zoë proclaimed appreciatively, "let's just say your sister is one hell of a good shot."

"And, thank goodness the suspect wasn't," Carmen emphasized with a nervous laugh.

"Stop pulling his leg, Carmen." Chris remarked gravely. "If you hadn't shot that guy twice in the head, both Zoë and I would probably be dead right now."

"That's my sister," Roy replied, impressed by Carmen's abilities. "Did you guys figure out what this psycho's motive was?"

"Not really," Zoë answered disappointedly. "There's an endless list of things that could have contributed to James' destructiveness."

"Like what?" Roy insisted, his curiosity not satisfied in the least by Zoë's passiveness.

"Abuse during childhood, ridiculed as a teenager, devastated by his first love. . ." Zoë rattled off evenly. "Or, he was just your average kid who grew up in a good loving home, but was evil to the core."

"There isn't some scientific explanation for why these psychotics are the way they are?" Adrian inquired bewildered.

"Criminologists and forensic psychologists are relentlessly searching for that very answer," Carmen declared as she leaned forward giving Roy a hug.

"They need to step up their efforts," Adrian replied.

Roy swung his leg easily over the motorcycle seat and started the engine. He looked over at Carmen and patted the seat behind him. "Do you need a ride home?" he offered.

"I'll catch a ride with Zoë," Carmen replied, her face reddening. "Thanks, anyway."

"Adrian," Roy said, "do you want a ride?"

"Are you kidding?" Adrian asked sarcastically, rushing over and taking a seat behind him. "I'm always game for a ride."

"Who's going to ride with me?" Chris whined, crossing his arms.

"You'll be okay, partner," Carmen reassured him. She gave Roy a peck on the cheek and another hug. She pressed her lips against his ear. "Thank you for everything," she whispered.

"Anytime," Roy replied with a dismissive wave.

Roy raised his right hand in a two-finger salute and pulled away from the curb. Carmen watched as he popped a wheelie for Adrian's sheer enjoyment. Chris put his hand firmly on Carmen's shoulder, "I haven't had a chance to really thank you yet."

"It isn't necessary." Carmen remarked frankly. "We just got lucky this time."

"Not according to what Captain Davis whispered in my ear," Zoë interjected proudly. "He thinks you'll be promoted to captain some day soon."

"I wouldn't take it," Carmen stated thoughtfully. "I love being a homicide detective way too much."

∞

SAVAGE INHIBITIONS
Coming June 2006

160017

Made in the USA